WITHDRAWN

# GROUNDSWELL

ALSO BY KATIE LEE

*The Comfort Table*

*The Comfort Table:*
*Recipes for Everyday Occasions*

# GROUNDSWELL

WITHDRAWN NOVEL

## KATIE LEE

GALLERY BOOKS

New York London Toronto Sydney

Gallery Books
A Division of Simon & Schuster, Inc.
1230 Avenue of the Americas
New York, NY 10020

First Gallery Books hardcover edition June 2011

GALLERY BOOKS and colophon are registered trademarks of Simon & Schuster, Inc.

For information about special discounts for bulk purchases, please contact Simon & Schuster Special Sales at 1-866-506-1949 or business@simonandschuster.com.

The Simon & Schuster Speakers Bureau can bring authors to your live event. For more information or to book an event contact the Simon & Schuster Speakers Bureau at 1-866-248-3049 or visit our website at www.simonspeakers.com.

*Designed by Jaime Putorti*

Manufactured in the United States of America

10  9  8  7  6  5  4  3  2  1

Library of Congress Cataloging-in-Publication Data

Lee, Katie, 1981–
Groundswell: a novel/by Katie Lee.—1st Gallery Books hardcover ed.
p.  cm.
1. Women screenwriters—United States—Fiction. 2 Man-woman relationships—Fiction. 3. Surfing—Fiction. 4. Self-actualization (Psychology) in women—Fiction. I. Title.
PS3612.E3442G76  2011
813'.6—dc22
2010050796

ISBN 978-1-4391-8359-5
ISBN 978-1-4391-8369-4 (ebook)

} for Mc.S.

GROUNDSWELL (noun):

A perfectly even and balanced series

of waves, or swells, caused by a

distant storm or disturbance. Also

known as ideal surfing conditions.

For whatever we lose (like a you or a

me) it's always ourselves we find in

the sea.

—e.e. cummings

Fifth Avenue looked like a processional for a royal wedding, jammed with black Town Cars, Mercedes, and Maybachs. A sea of people behind metal barricades filled the sidewalk and the light of flashbulbs flickered just ahead.

As our car slowly approached the Metropolitan Museum of Art, I took a deep breath and rubbed my palms on the seat.

"You okay?" Garrett asked, tilting his head to look at me with an amused expression on his face. "You're not going to stroke out on me, are you?"

I gave him a half smile. "If I did, could I get out of going to the Met Gala tonight?"

"Anna Wintour would hunt you down, and if the stroke didn't kill you, she would do the job herself."

I laughed, picturing Anna Wintour prowling the Lenox

Hill emergency room, perfectly coiffed and carrying a Karl Lagerfeld–designed shotgun.

Garrett reached out for both of my hands and dried each sweaty palm on the trousers of his Tom Ford tuxedo. Only my husband, blockbuster movie star, could look debonair while blotting my sweaty palms. Then again, he pretty much looked good doing anything—driving, sleeping, changing the channel—didn't matter what, he just always looked good.

"Remember, Emma, I'm right here next to you. I've got your back. All you have to do is smile." And then he flashed me his trademark grin—slightly crooked, all charm.

I had been married to Garrett for seven years, and in that time I had gone from country bumpkin college dropout, to celebrity wife, to successful screenwriter. And I had Garrett Walker to thank for that. He'd fallen in love with me when I was a twenty-two-year-old production assistant on his latest movie, and before I knew it I was a fixture on his arm at every industry event. When I craved more career satisfaction, he helped me pursue my dream of screenwriting. And last year, my first screenplay became the smash hit of the summer. It was an unlikely love story about a handsome movie star who falls in love with a nobody. As the saying goes, write what you know.

Garrett's head of security was in the front passenger seat, and he'd already phoned in our position to Met security. The driver put the car in park and walked around to open my door. With each car, the crowd and photographers hushed momentarily while they waited to see which celebrity would emerge. I stepped out as Garrett slid across the seat, and the second he popped out behind me, the crowd exploded in cheers and cameras flashed with blinding ferocity. Women screamed at the top of their lungs, some had signs reading, "I love you Garrett," and I even saw a few of them crying.

My heartbeat quickened again. I forced myself to smile and hoped no one could see my lips trembling. You'd think I'd be used to this by now, but somehow I wasn't. Events like this felt like running the gauntlet of criticism in slow motion. No matter how beautiful my dress, someone would write something nasty about it tomorrow.

Garrett didn't have to worry about that. He was completely at ease. He buttoned his tuxedo jacket, and then looked up, grinning ear to ear. God, his confidence amazed me. That's what made me fall for him in the first place. He raised his arm into the air, waving to his horde of fans, sending them into even more of a frenzy. He was just Garrett, my husband—the guy who sat around in his pajamas and drank coffee with me while we read the papers, the guy who sweated next to me while we ran on the treadmill, the guy who ate popcorn with me while we sat in bed and watched bad TV. But to these people, he was Garrett Walker, the biggest movie star in the world.

Garrett rested his palm—his dry, steady, reassuring palm—on the small of my back for a moment before pulling me close to him. Then he pulled away, waving his hand up and down my body like a game show girl displaying a prize, and nodded to the crowd before taking my hand in his and making our way to the anxiously awaiting photographers and microphone-wielding television reporters. The press line on both sides of the endless steps looked a mile long. We stopped for the first grouping and posed as the photographers yelled, trying to get us to look at each of their cameras. As always, it was an out-of-body experience—all I could hear was "Garrett, Garrett, Garrett, over here!" and "Emma, Emma, Emma, look here!" It felt as if an epileptic seizure were coming on from staring too long into a strobe light.

"Emma, give him a kiss!" one of them yelled. I stood on my tiptoes and gave him a smooch on the cheek, sending the photographers into overdrive. They always loved the kiss shots. Garrett gave me his big smile, feigning a surprised look, and kissed me back. That would be the one in the *New York Post* tomorrow.

Now it was time for the TV crews. Thankfully, they usually aired only the clips of Garrett talking. Our first stop was Maria Menounos with *Access Hollywood*.

"It looked like a lovefest between the two of you out there on the red carpet this evening. As one of Hollywood's most happily married couples, how do you keep the romance alive?" she asked.

"Well, Maria, just look at my beautiful wife," Garrett said. "I am the luckiest guy here tonight. But you know, most important, it's about honesty and trust. We're partners."

"Speaking of partners, Emma, your film, *Fame Tax*, was the big hit last summer," Maria said. "When can we expect something new from you?"

My publicist would have my hide if I looked like a stunned deer on network television, and I felt my lips moving on autopilot. "I'm working on a new screenplay now, and we're hoping to start production in the fall."

"And Garrett, will you be producing this film as well?" Maria continued.

"Oh, no," he said. "The great Harvey Weinstein has his mitts on this one. I can't afford her anymore." He smiled at me lovingly, and I smiled back, wishing I'd remembered to take a beta blocker.

We walked through the doors into the massive Great Hall of the Met and I felt instant relief. All the posing was over . . . until I remembered: The posing is never over. The magnitude of the ball always stunned me—each year Anna Wintour outdid the previous, with every major celebrity in attendance. Everywhere you looked there was one person more famous than the next, all phenomenally dressed. It was rumored that Anna's office kept a spreadsheet of what each guest would be wearing, from her dress to her earrings to her shoes and bag. Even though I'd spent weeks making fun of my friend Michael for acting like my ensemble was such a big deal, I was relieved he'd taken charge. To borrow his words, my dress was "correct."

Garrett was in his element. Even in a room filled with celebrities, he was the biggest star. We waited in the reception line to greet Anna and the other hosts of the evening before making our way through the Egyptian wing to the Temple of Dendur for dinner.

"Honey, look, there's Lily up ahead," I said. "Let's catch up to her—I haven't seen her all week." Lily was an actress and one of my oldest friends. Lately, she had been alternating between bigger parts in independent films and best friend roles in more commercial movies.

"You'll see Lily inside," Garrett said. "Let's take our time. This is my favorite room at the museum. Besides, we never get to come here during the day." What he meant was, *he* could never come here during the day without disrupting multiple field trips with his mere presence. I had no problem blending in.

I gave his arm a squeeze. "Okay, you revel in the art, I've got to make a pit stop," I said, fixing his tie. Then I headed to the bathroom, which was already as much of a scene as the event itself. Naomi Campbell was typing away on her Black-Berry, Vera Wang was helping Jennifer Garner with her zipper, and a group of young models (whose faces I recognized but names I didn't know) were smoking cigarettes.

My feet were already killing me. These shoes that Michael made me wear were miniature torture chambers. I felt like I was having my feet bound. Whoever said that designer stilet-tos could be comfortable was a big liar—or never walked any-where. I got a spot in front of the mirror and opened my bag to get my lip gloss. I felt my iPhone buzz. It was a text from Lily.

Meet me in the auditorium in five.

Hmm, must be serious. Otherwise Lily wouldn't miss a sec-ond of the biggest event of the season to meet me now in an empty auditorium. She should be out chatting up every Hol-lywood power player in the room. This was her favorite day of the year, like Christmas and her birthday rolled into one.

I stared at Lily's text a beat longer, and then I realized this wasn't my phone. My iPhone's wallpaper was a silly picture of Garrett that I took on our last beach vacation, and his phone had a picture of me that he took that same afternoon. And here onscreen was my happy, sand-streaked face looking back at me. We must have switched phones in our hurry to leave the apartment that evening.

I looked up and caught my reflection in the mirror—and saw on my face the sick feeling I had in my gut. There had to be some explanation. Maybe Lily meant to text me and hit his number by accident. At that moment I should have found Garrett, handed back his phone, and asked him why Lily wanted to see him so urgently. But a knot of suspicion grew where the nausea had been, and something told me that wasn't the way to find out the truth, that the only way to know what was going on here was to watch and wait. I knew Garrett's phone would buzz again if I didn't open Lily's text. So I decided to see what Garrett would do when he discovered the message.

It was always easy to find Garrett in a crowd—you just followed the chum. I weaved through the crush of silk and tuxedos, and when I was back on his arm, I handed him his phone. "Hey hon, I think we switched phones."

"Oops, here's yours," he said, slipping it out of his inner breast pocket, and then returning his own to the same spot.

"Garrett, there's a producer over there I should say hello to. I'll be back in a minute." I tried to settle my face into an expression that looked normal. Garrett kissed my cheek and then I walked away, toward my conversation with an imaginary producer. Slipping back through the crowd, I turned to watch as Garrett plucked his phone from his pocket and glanced at it. Then I watched as he set off purposefully for the auditorium. I grabbed a glass of champagne from the tray of a passing waitress, downed it in one full swig, and set off after him.

The doors to the auditorium were open, so I slid silently into a shadowy alcove. Down the aisle from me, with her back turned, was Lily—the girl I'd known for years, with whom I'd shared rent, heartbreaks, and every up and down of my adult life. And nestled into the small of her back was Garrett's hand as he drew her closer and whispered into her ear. As if on cue, she threw back her long, blond hair—the classic bed-head move that she'd perfected years ago and that only meant one thing. She glanced down at the deep V of her dress and stepped toward him, just enough for her perfect breasts to graze his chest suggestively. He slid his hand over her ass and she turned coyly to walk away, until he pulled her back toward him and kissed her passionately.

I rocked back on my heels, and caught myself from falling at the last possible second. My husband—my white knight for the last seven years—was cheating on me with my best friend. And my unlikely love story was over.

# PART ONE

## 2002

1

"God, my feet are killing me," I said. "I hate this job. At least the waitstaff gets to wear comfortable shoes. I have to hustle around that restaurant all night in heels and a short skirt."

Lily was only half listening to me, twirling her hair while she flipped the pages of *Vogue*.

"You won't believe what this creep did to me tonight," I continued. "I told him the wait for a table would be about forty-five minutes. And he said he'd make it worth my while if I bumped him and his skanky girlfriend up on the list. Of course, I could use a good tip, so I seated them right away. I hand him his menu and he puts out his hand. I think he's slipping me a twenty, but no. He gives me a tube of some sort of cream and leans into my ear and tells me he holds the patent on female Viagra and to have a little fun with my boyfriend tonight."

"Perv," Lily mumbled.

"I handed it right back to him and said, sweet as pie, 'Honey, one look at you and I know your girlfriend probably needs this more than me.'"

"Ha!" Lily ripped a page out of the magazine and held it up for me to see. "Look," she said. "It's me!"

I took the page from her hand and looked at the picture of Lily wearing a short, silver-sequined party dress, her head tossed back with her perfectly imperfect blond hair falling over the left side of her face, her pouty lips slightly parted, revealing her big white smile. I'd be lying if I didn't admit that I felt a twinge of envy. This was the kind of stuff that always happened to Lily.

While I was standing on my feet for hours, contending with herds of pissed-off, self-important, hungry New Yorkers, my roommate was out at a fabulous cocktail party lauding the designer of the moment, while wearing his dress and having her photo taken for the pages of the biggest fashion magazine in the world.

It's not that I wanted to be Lily. But I did want to be a success. And my chosen profession was screenwriting. I knew I needed on-set experience and a real understanding of the process of filmmaking, so I had sent out a million résumés for internships with film companies, but so far no one wanted me—not even for free. I was struggling to support myself as a restaurant hostess, and Lily was already making it as an aspiring actress. She'd just been cast in a smallish part in a film by the most buzzed-about indie director and she was going to parties with the kind of people who had their pictures in *Vogue*. Scratch that. She *was* the kind of person who had her picture in *Vogue*. Granted, the picture was tiny, and the caption was even tinier, but still. She was on her way.

I would never, ever have said it out loud, but Lily had it easier than I did. Her family had money, and let's face it: Money makes everything easier. While I worked, Lily's parents supported her financially so she could go on auditions. My mother barely scraped by herself, and my dad was long gone.

Dad left after Mom found out he was cheating. The news was delivered to her in a call from the bank, telling her that a check had bounced. I was only eight and my sister was thirteen. Mom packed us both into the car and went down to the bank to have a look for herself. They showed her a whole series of canceled checks made out to cash, and the real kicker: a zero balance. My dad worked late and traveled, and I guess my mother must have already had her suspicions. When she confronted him later that night, he confessed on the spot that he'd been having an affair with a woman who lived a few towns away. He didn't even bother to pack up his possessions. One minute he was there, and the next he wasn't, and that was the last time I saw him.

My dad had never been much of a provider, but after he left, things got even harder for Mom. My grandparents lived nearby, so they could babysit while she worked, and we ate dinner over there most nights. I didn't realize until later that we ate there so often because my mom couldn't afford to feed us. If it weren't for my grandparents, we would have been on welfare.

Those years took their toll on Mom. When I left Kentucky for college in Manhattan, she supported me all the way, took me to the airport and waved goodbye, tears running down her face. The last thing she said to me was "You can always come back." She left the rest of that sentence unsaid, but I knew what she really meant: You can always come back . . .

*when you fail.* Mom always believed that no matter how good things might seem, they were bound to explode in your face. And I couldn't really blame her—after all, nothing much had gone her way. But although I knew there was a home for me in Kentucky, and my mother would welcome me back with open arms, failure was not an option for me. I'd stick it out in New York if I had to eat cat food.

Lily was the first person I met when I came to New York my freshman year of college. She had the kind of confidence that made her stand out in any room—especially a dorm room. I got to our room first and I'd already unpacked my clothes and made my bed when she swept in, smelling faintly of cigarette smoke and perfume. Her hair was long and wavy and it looked naturally kissed by the sun. (I found out later that those highlights were bought and paid for, but they looked real enough to me.) And she wore an outfit that was casually assembled yet perfect, and to this day I couldn't replicate it if I tried. I was older than Lily, because I'd spent a year after high school working to save money for school. But you wouldn't have known by looking at us that I was the older one. Lily intimidated me on sight—everything about her was stylish. I looked sidelong at my stack of Levis, T-shirts, and cardigans and knew I was out of my league.

Lily always laughed when she described how I looked that first day of college—terrified, excited—in direct contrast with her own blasé sophistication. But she took me under her wing from the first moment we met. She was from New Jersey and had been sneaking out to nightclubs in Manhattan since she was sixteen, so she already traveled in a circle of friends several years older than her. She knew the bouncer or bartender at every hot club, and she'd dress me up and drag me along.

Soon she accepted that I wasn't much of a partier. But our friendship survived that blow, and when she was discovered by a casting director our sophomore year and promptly dropped out, I was happy for her. When her parents found her an apartment and she offered to spring me from dorm life and rent me half her place for far less than half the rent, I moved in right away. We'd been inseparable ever since.

"Oh my God, Lily," I said. "Look, there's Mikey in the background!" Sure enough, just behind Lily in the *Vogue* picture was the unmistakably fashionable outline of my other closest friend, Michael. Lily and I had met him at a party. He had been leaning against a wall, dressed in an ascot and holding a pipe. Of course, he was also only twenty years old at the time, so the look was more comical than sophisticated. He took one glance at Lily and decided she was a friend worth cultivating, and he grudgingly accepted me as a third wheel, but we'd grown closer since then. I knew that within all those layers of couture aspiration lay a sweet soul with just as many insecurities as I had. I also knew that he'd grown up in a town just as Podunk as mine.

"It's not 'Mikey,' it's Michael," Lily snapped. "If he ever wants to be taken seriously in fashion, he can't go around being called Mikey or even Mike, for that matter. I told him only 'Michael' from now on."

I rolled my eyes. "Whatever."

"What are you doing tonight? Want to go out with me?" Lily asked.

"Lily, the thought of putting on shoes right now and screaming over loud music makes me want to vomit," I said. "I've worked every late shift this week, and tomorrow is my only day off. I don't want to sleep through it."

"Come on, Emma, you never come out with me anymore," she protested in a whiny voice.

"Lily—"

"Fine, Granny," she cut me off. "But you have zero chance of meeting a guy staying home and watching reruns of *Golden Girls.*"

I laughed. "Too true. Consider it my homework—if I'm going to be a great screenwriter some day, I should at least study the most popular sitcom of all time."

"Suit yourself, Estelle."

Lily let the door clang shut behind her, leaving a cloud of perfume and hair spray in her wake, and I curled up on the couch.

I didn't know what to do with myself in the quiet apartment. There was no need to study anymore. After hanging on to my scholarship by my fingernails, I ultimately lost my battle with the ill-fated science requirement a few weeks ago. Sayonara, scholarship . . . arrivederci, diploma . . . buh-bye, dreams. Yep, geology was my Waterloo.

Every day in class had been a terror. I tried to listen, tried to focus, but soon the drone of the professor's voice and the sheer fright of failing made my brain shut down. I should have been rising to the occasion and conquering the challenge. Instead I flailed and sank like the *Titanic.*

There was a little relief in having the failure behind me. I still had anxiety dreams about forgotten term papers, but now I could reassure myself when I woke up that those days were over. There was only one remaining nugget of dread nestled in the pit of my stomach: I hadn't yet told my mom that I'd lost my scholarship. So many times I'd wanted to tell her, then didn't. She'd only feel obligated to help me fix it, but there was nothing she could do. And there was no one else I could confide in. My older sister, Maureen, would derive too much pleasure from giving me an earful about how irresponsible I was. The one upside of all this is that I wouldn't have to buy her a Christmas gift in a few months—my failure would be the best present I could ever give her. I couldn't call Grace, either. She was my best friend from home, and my partner in crime ever since we were kids. She'd been dying to get out of Kentucky as long as I had. The year I'd spent working after high school, we'd been side by side folding T-shirts at the local strip mall. Unlike me, though, she was still back there and dating her high school boyfriend. She'd kick my ass if she knew I'd let "Rocks for Jocks" get the better of me. Only I could ace a graduate-level semiotics class and still manage to fail Geology 101.

I peeled myself off the couch and began to gather my laundry. Lily's side of the bedroom was a mess, a mound of rejected clothes in a heap in the center of her twin bed, while my side was perfectly neat. I was a firm believer that everything had its place. I was past letting her untidiness annoy me; after all, dealing with her clutter was much better than the alternative—I'd never be able to afford rent in Manhattan. I stripped out of my black knit dress, noticing that it smelled vaguely of garlic and Parmesan cheese, tossed it in the laundry bag, and changed into my "uniform" of a wife-beater and sweatpants. So much better . . . I'd wear sweatpants everywhere if it was socially acceptable.

The elevator always took forever in our building and I stood in the hallway waiting for its doors to open. I watched the buttons slowly light up as the elevator went up each floor, and glanced down the hall toward 9E, praying the doorknob wouldn't move. "Cute Neighbor Boy," as Lily and I liked to call him, lived there.

Finally the bell rang and the ninth floor button lit up. Just as I was stepping inside, Cute Neighbor Boy opened the door to his apartment. I practically threw myself at the DOOR CLOSE button. I could hear my mother's voice in my head, "Never wear sweatpants in public. You never know who you're going to run into."

## 2

I woke up on the sofa with a start, an hour after I'd set my alarm, which was beeping unattended in the bedroom. Lily was passed out in her bed. The girl could sleep through an asteroid collision.

I had to get down to the restaurant to pick up my paycheck and deposit it before noon to make sure my rent check wouldn't bounce. I knew that Lily was unlikely to cash it right away. She hardly needed the money. But it was a point of pride for me never to be late, and never to take her wealth for granted. I got in the shower and didn't have time to dry my hair, so I slicked it back into a bun. I put on a sweatshirt that I'd customized by cutting off the collar, some designer jeans that Lily had bought me for my birthday, and wrapped a scarf around my neck. It wasn't high fashion but it was a far cry from the dorky mom jeans I used to wear with my running shoes.

As I waited for the elevator, there was a slam down the hall and I glanced up to see Cute Neighbor Boy locking his door. When the elevator came, I extended my arm to hold the door, making a bit of a show of it, just in case he'd busted me in my braless getup the night before and knew that I'd made a quick escape. Lily and I were always creating scenarios about him, but as of yet, I hadn't had the guts to say hello to him. Not that it mattered. Nothing good could come out of hooking up with your neighbor. I repeated this universal truth to myself while he and I rode silently down to the first floor, and I gave him a weak smile before racing out of our building.

Still at a clip, I walked down the street to the deli. "Bacon, egg, and American cheese on a plain bagel, please," I told the counter guy. This was my favorite place because the coffee was self-serve, so you could start mainlining caffeine even before you'd paid for breakfast.

I stood at the counter, sipping life back into my veins, when I heard a man's raspy voice. "Hey, don't you live in my building?"

Even though I'd never heard Cute Neighbor Boy's voice, it was exactly what I'd imagined he'd sound like. I turned around, and sure enough it was him. I managed to stutter out a "yes," totally flustered by his blue eyes and thick dark hair. All I could think was, thank God I put on mascara this morning. I realized he was talking, but I wasn't hearing anything, only watching his lips move. They were full and kissable, very kissable.

"Hey, lady, bacon-egg-and-cheese on plain is ready!" the man behind the counter yelled at me.

I took my bagel and sheepishly turned back around to Cute Neighbor Boy. "I'm Sam," he said.

"Emma," I said, wiping the grease from the bagel wrapper on my jeans before stretching out my hand.

"We should get together sometime," he said. "You live with that blond girl, right? Isn't she an actress?"

Oh. So that's it. He wasn't interested in me, he was interested in Lily. Shocker. "Yeah, I do," I said, suddenly sullen. "You mean, like, the three of us?"

"No," he said quickly. "I mean, she could come along if she wants. I have an art show in Brooklyn tonight. Here's a flyer if you and your friend want to come. Or just you."

So maybe he was actually interested in me? I couldn't really tell—he had a certain cultivated mysteriousness about him—just the right amount of restraint to seduce any girl. You know, the kind of guy who looks at you for just a beat too long, who says he should get going right when the tension's at its thickest. "Sure," I said, trying to sound nonchalant. "I'll try to stop by."

"Cool."

~~~~~~

"The F train goes to DUMBO, right?" I called out to Mikey, who was in the kitchen, pouring himself a drink while I got dressed. I'm embarrassed to admit how relieved I was when I found out Lily had plans that evening and couldn't come with me to the art show.

"How should I know?" he responded. "I couldn't tell you the last time I went to Brooklyn. And I'm pretty sure I took a cab."

"How much money do you think you spend on taxis in a year?" The guy works five blocks from his apartment and takes a cab to work.

"I know," he said, biting his lip as if admitting a bad habit. "But think of all the money I'm saving by not having to resole my Gucci loafers every three months. I have to look after my investments."

When he walked into the bedroom with a glass in each hand, he paused and looked me up and down. "And what do we have going on here? Special, Emms, real special."

"You don't like my outfit?" I asked.

"No. Ew. No. Take off the scarf and that enormous cocktail ring," he ordered. "Here take this," he said, handing me a glass. "You look like you need it."

Mikey put his hand under his chin, in a "thinking man" position, as he studied my outfit. "I actually like the dress . . . it's vintage, right?" He didn't wait for an answer. "It looks a little Marc Jacobs-ish. I could do without those shoes, though. I think we need a boot. Yes, that's it. We need a boot. Do you have a boot?"

Before I responded, he was digging through my half of the closet, throwing shoes out behind him as he looked for just the right pair.

"Aha! Try these," he said.

I put on the boots, a little unsure of what he was going for, but Mikey always got it right. Even if I didn't particularly like what he put me in, I ended up getting compliments from everyone else.

"Yes! That's perfect!" he said, very pleased with himself. "Now you just need to part your hair down the center and you'll be Ali MacGraw in *Love Story*. Okay, let's go find your

Sam. Just don't be heartbroken if it turns out he likes me more than you. He *is* suspiciously hot. It might not be you *or* Lily he's after . . . I'm just saying."

"You think every hot guy is gay," I said. He raised his eyebrows, and I said nothing more. Mikey's gaydar was notoriously fallible. On the way out, I reached for my navy blue peacoat on the coatrack as we were walking out the front door.

"Don't even think about it!" Mikey snapped.

"But it's chilly—"

"Freeze for fashion, Emms, freeze for fashion," he said.

After successfully convincing Mikey to take the subway to Brooklyn, I realized he was right about the outfit—I was getting plenty of stares and some hipster-looking girl told me she liked my boots—to which Mikey shot me a told-you-so smirk.

After taking a few wrong turns, Mikey and I found the address listed on the flyer on a quiet, deserted cobblestone street. It looked like a big warehouse, not an art studio. "This is it," I said to Mikey, but it came out sounding more like a question than a statement. Mikey looked at me skeptically.

We went into the dark hallway and saw a pink piece of paper with an arrow drawn on it. We followed and found another pink flyer by the elevator with the number 3. The elevator had a metal gate that I pulled closed, and it slowly creaked up to the third floor, then the door opened to a loud, rocking party. I pulled open the gate and gave Mikey my best impersonation of his told-you-so smirk.

The massive loft was filled with a mixed crowd of young professionals in tailored suits, hipsters with nose piercings and spiky hair, and modelish Lily look-alikes. It was a raw space, beams and pipes exposed, with brick walls. A DJ was spinning in a booth set up in the corner, and art lined each of the walls.

Mikey looked around approvingly. "Chicness, Emms."

"Want to walk around and take a look at the art?" I asked.

"Um, you take a walk around and look at the art, and I'm going to take a walk right over there and take a look at that," he said, pointing to a handsome Wall Street–type guy in a suit.

"You think he's gay?"

"Puh-lease," he said. "Too-da-loo, doll face."

I wished I had a little of his confidence. He had no problem just walking up to a stranger and starting a conversation. In his place, I'd just stand there stuttering to get one coherent sentence out of my mouth. I'm still shocked I was able to have a conversation with Sam this morning. Come to think of it, though, I didn't really say much, just sort of grunted hello and nice to meet you. He probably wished he hadn't invited me after that. This place was so crowded, though, maybe I wouldn't even run into him.

I strolled around, trying my best to feel like I belonged in the sea of impossibly hip art people, and stopped to see each painting while cultivating an air of contemplation. I was looking at a white canvas with some black brushstrokes that looked vaguely like the shape of a woman when I felt a hand placed on the small of my back. I turned around expecting to see Mikey, but instead I was met by the gaze of two big blue eyes, a head of black curly hair, and a warm smile.

"Hey," Sam said.

"Oh, hi," I said, trying my best not to look startled.

"That's one of my paintings," he said, pointing at the sort-of woman figure.

"I love it," I lied. "It's very mysterious. Kind of haunting."

"It's funny you should say that," he said.

"I'm sorry," I said. "Did I say something wrong?"

"Oh no, it's just that—" he paused. "You sort of inspired it."

"Me?" I said incredulously.

"Well, the mystery of you," he said. "I'd see you in the building sometimes." He stammered and continued. "I think you're really beautiful, but I'd never talked to you . . . until this morning."

"Are you sorry you ruined the mystery?" I asked. Funny, just that morning I'd thought that about him—that he seemed very mysterious. And here he was telling me he'd felt the same way about me.

"Not at all . . ." And there it was: the stare with a quarter smile held a beat too long. This guy was good.

"Gosh, I'm really flattered," I said. "I can honestly say I've never inspired a painting before, or anything, really, for that matter."

"Maybe we could get together sometime?" he asked. "You know, like not at a big crowded art show?"

"Sure."

"Okay, I'll see you in the elevator," he said. "I have to go try to sell something—you know, gotta pay the rent."

He leaned down and kissed me on the cheek and turned to walk away, looking over his shoulder once and giving me a mischievous grin. Yep, he was good, all right. I hoped he couldn't tell my mouth was open in shock.

I found Mikey in the same spot I'd left him—talking to the Wall Street guy, who definitely didn't look gay to me. I knew Mikey could see me approaching from the corner of his eye, but he pretended not to notice until I was standing at his elbow.

"Hello," I said, with a demure southern lilt. Whenever I put on my "Tara" voice, it was my cue to Mikey that it was time to go.

"Well, look who it is," he said, as if he were surprised to see me. "Don't you look pleased with yourself?"

"Aren't you going to introduce me to your friend?" I said, nodding toward the Wall Street guy.

"Emma, this is Malcolm. He works at Goldman Sachs."

"Very nice to meet you," Malcolm said, looking a little uncomfortable. "Do you know where the bathroom is?"

Neither of us did, and Malcolm set off to find it.

"I told you he wasn't gay," I said to Mikey. "He was wearing a wedding ring, for crying out loud."

"Are you that naïve, Emma?" Mikey said. "Do you know how many married guys in finance hit on me? You scared him off."

"Whatever," I said. "You ready to go? I'm tired."

"Emma," he said, drawing my name out and looking down at me with disappointment, his cue that he wanted to stay. "You always want to go home so early. Stop being such a grandma. You got all dressed up to go out, now show it off." He looked around. "But you're right that we're done here. We should go to this new place I heard about in the East Village. We can meet up with Lily." I agreed, if only just to get him headed toward the subway.

"Okay, Mikey," I said later, as we were walking up the subway stairs to Houston Street, "I'm going home. You go meet Lily and have fun."

"Emma!" he said, pleading. "You tricked me!"

"Granny needs her beauty rest."

~~~~~

I got back to the apartment, kicked off my boots, and immediately changed into my sweats. I made a cup of hot tea, turned on the television, and opened my laptop. I waited for it to connect to the Internet and logged into my email account. There were a couple new ones, one from my friend Grace.

Then my computer made the ping noise of a new email. The subject line read, "URGENT: PA Position," and I clicked on it.

Hi Emma,

I work with the LA-based production company Feature House. A few months back you sent us your résumé seeking an internship position. We didn't have a spot for you then, but I've just been informed that one of our paid PAs has to leave the New York set of the new Mark Lynch film, and now we're shorthanded. We're scheduled to wrap before Christmas and we'd need you to start right away. If you're interested, email your reply immediately, and report to the Manhattan set tomorrow at 6:30 a.m. Further location details to follow.

Regards,
Sue Duncan

My hands shook as I read the email. Oh my God. I would have leapt at any opportunity right now, but the new Mark Lynch movie—this was huge. He was one of the most successful action film directors in the business. His last few films had been massive, and not just popular but also well reviewed. There was nothing to think about. I hit REPLY.

Dear Sue,

Thank you for your email. I enthusiastically accept. Just tell me where to be.

Best wishes,
Emma Guthrie

By this point it was midnight, far too late to call Mom. Besides, it would still require telling her that I dropped out of school, and I wasn't ready for that conversation. I could call Mikey or Lily, but that would mean shouting at them over the din of whatever club they were in, and that held no appeal at the moment.

There was a soft knock on the door. That was odd. If Lily forgot her keys she was usually a lot noisier than that. And New York isn't the kind of town where visitors stop by unannounced. Startled, I tiptoed to the door and looked through the peephole. Thick black hair, bright blue eyes, mischievous grin. It was Sam. My heart fluttered as I pulled open the door.

He smiled. "Well, hello."

## 3

The sky was still dark when I let myself out of Sam's apartment. God, he was beautiful when he slept. I had memorized every outline of his face, every eyelash, because of course, I hadn't slept at all. I felt shaky with excitement over Sam, disbelief over last night, and lack of sleep. I wrote him a quick note—*Headed to work, talk later?*

I showered quickly and threw on my Manhattan uniform—the same jeans and scarf combination I always wore. I had no idea what PAs wore, but I figured I'd be on my feet all day so comfort was important. And my job was so insignificant that no one would care what I looked like. I grabbed my peacoat (so there, Mikey) and headed out to my first day on the job.

I was early for my 6:30 a.m. call time, but the set—a quiet street in the West Village—was already humming with activity.

Large white trailers lined one side, and PAs with clipboards, earpieces, and walkie-talkies zipped around. I'd been told to report to Stacy Leverett, the second assistant director, who was in charge of all the PAs. Sue Duncan told me she had auburn hair and always wore black, but I wouldn't have needed the description to find Stacy. She looked the same age as the PAs, but there was something world-weary about her, and instead of scurrying around, she was the one barking the orders.

Stacy looked me over top to bottom in a way that made me feel clinically examined. She snapped into her walkie-talkie, "I need Jen. Now." She glanced back at me. "Jen's going to show you the ropes."

Before Stacy had even finished her sentence, a young woman appeared at her side. She was a few inches shorter than me, but what she lacked in height, she made up for in attitude. Her features were sharp and her eyes were dark and serious, punctuated by one pierced eyebrow. Her hair looked like she'd cut it in the dark. It wasn't so much asymmetrical as haphazard, and it was pitch-black except for a streak of platinum blond in her bangs, which she kept aggressively raking out of her face. She wore a loose flannel shirt and a hoodie over wrecked jeans. She looked exactly like half the students in my film editing class at NYU, so I felt right at home.

I followed Jen around like an obedient puppy, and she warmed up after a few minutes. She didn't crack a smile but seemed to enjoy filling me in, and I decided to make like a sponge and absorb everything she had to say.

"First thing you need to know: There are two kinds of PAs. There are the PAs who do crowd control. That's me," Jen said. "And there are the PAs who make copies and fetch coffee. That, apparently, is you. You take your orders from Stacy.

Somebody else tells you to do something? Ask Stacy first. People are bossy on set, so you need to know who the real bosses are. The big boss is Mark Lynch, of course. But you stay out of his way unless you're handing him a script or a cup of coffee. Got it?"

I nodded, and she started pointing out the various trailers. "That's Garrett Walker's trailer. He's on set today. So crowd control is gonna be a pain in my ass. You should see the women who line up just to get a look at him. Don't be fooled by their tears and sweet faces. They're vicious. They will cut you to get near him."

I started to laugh, assuming she was joking. The dark expression on Jen's face stopped me. She wasn't joking.

"Craft services is over there. That's where most of the set will eat. The stars usually eat in their trailers. They don't mingle." Then Jen looked me over the same way Stacy had.

This was getting weird. "Jen, is there something wrong with how I'm dressed?"

Jen sighed. "All right, look. Stacy asked me to show you around for a reason. I mean, she knows I'll give it to you straight. There's a certain kind of young female PA that the guys on set like to call a 'victim.' You don't want to be a victim."

I must have looked as confused as I felt, because Jen elaborated. "Victims are cute girls, all right? And certain stars have a reputation for liking certain types. Garrett Walker happens to like tall, slender, fresh-faced brunettes. Like you. Garrett's a good-looking guy—if you like your men clean-cut." Jen made it clear that she did not. "So when he's nice to you, you're going to want to be nice right back. But keep it professional. And whatever you do, don't go into his trailer."

"Oh my God, you mean . . ."

"No, no, don't get me wrong. Garrett's a nice guy. But don't kid yourself. He's not going to marry you, and when he's moved on—which he will—you'll have a big *V* for victim stamped on your forehead. And then you have to live with that for the rest of production. You don't want that." Jen had a concerned look on her face, and her hard demeanor had gone a little soft at the edges.

"Listen," I said, "the last thing I'm looking for here is a husband, and the last place I'd go looking for one is in Garrett Walker's trailer. Working on this set is a dream come true for me. I just want to do a good job."

"Good." Jen actually smiled. "You'll do fine."

~~~~~~~

I laughed a little at the thought that Garrett Walker would be interested in me. He was the perfect American male in one movie star package, and he didn't date real women with flaws who ate bagel sandwiches for breakfast. He dated Brazilian models, or he dated no one. He had a smile that made grown women melt or weep or faint—or according to Jen, threaten physical violence. And his body was legendary. It was his big brown eyes that I found irresistible—and the way they twinkled a bit when he smiled, as if he had a little spark machine in his head. On top of that, he was known for stopping his car to help some stranger fix a flat tire, or to rescue a lost dog. He was too good to be true, really—a Hollywood creation. He was the kind of guy you admired from a distance, but you never got close to, and that was just fine by me.

Jen set me up with my own headset and walkie-talkie and gave me a quick lesson in how to use them. Then she told me it was my job to stand on the perimeter of filming and wait for orders. This time of morning, there would be a lot of orders for coffee, and there also might be some script changes from the night before. I'd have to be quick on my feet.

There was a feeling of unreality about everything that day. I suppose it's that way on the first day of any new job, but this was magnified to a power of ten. This was a new job on a Hollywood film set and everything seemed intensely scary and yet weirdly familiar. I'd catch sight of someone I thought I knew, and then realize that it was the guy who'd won best supporting actor a few years ago for that football movie. And the scene itself was like something out of a dream—the lights, the barked orders, the frenzy. It was incredibly strange and beyond exciting.

"Emma, I need you to pick up script changes and take them to the assistant director." It was Stacy's voice talking into my ear. I clicked my walkie-talkie. "I'm on it." Was that the right thing to say? It sounded right. Or maybe I'd watched too many cop shows. Jen had already told me where to pick up script changes, and I was there and back in a flash. The assistant director was a pudgy young guy with sunglasses pushed up on his head. He didn't even glance at me when he took the changes, much less say thank you. And then I looked up. Garrett Walker was on the set, and he was looking in our direction. And he smiled.

Involuntarily, I looked around to see what he was smiling at. Then I looked back. Now he was laughing. The assistant director snapped at me. "You can go now."

I scurried back to my position. A few minutes passed, and I heard Stacy's voice in my ear again. "Dave, Garrett wants his cappuccino." I saw a young guy run off to craft services and come back faster than I would have thought possible, then maneuver his way through the set to bring Garrett his coffee. Garrett looked at Dave, then said something to the assistant director. The director overheard and rolled his eyes.

Stacy's voice clicked in my ear again. "Garrett says he wanted an iced cappuccino. Emma, would you bring Garrett his *iced* cappuccino?"

*Holy shit.* I booked to craft services and begged the first caterer I saw to make me an iced cappuccino just the way Garrett liked it. The guy looked me up and down and smirked. "He never drinks iced. We just sent him his cap, extra hot— the way he always drinks it."

I shook my head. "He doesn't want it anymore. He wants iced."

My heart was racing as I willed him to hurry up. When he finally handed it over, he said, "Have fun." His voice was insinuating, and I really didn't like the sound of it.

I ran back to the set and slowed down just in time to pick my way through lights, chairs, and people to get to Garrett. He was chatting with Mark Lynch, who looked like an overgrown teenager—unkempt hair, concert T, jeans, and Converse All-Stars. Garrett seemed to belong to a different species—he cast his own light. I stood there for a second waiting for a pause in their conversation, and Garrett looked up and smiled at me. "There you are. Thanks, love, just what I needed. That guy never gets my coffee right." Then he winked at me. It should have been ridiculous—I mean, who winks? My grandfather doesn't even wink at me. But suddenly I felt light-headed. I don't think I even spoke. I just nodded and got away from there as fast as I could.

Once filming began, the tone of the set changed and

became even more intense. Before I knew it, hours had passed and then the set broke for lunch. It wasn't until that moment that I realized my entire body had been coiled. My shoulders were up around my ears and even my calves were flexed. I walked toward craft services thinking I might grab some coffee and a sandwich, when I heard Stacy's voice in my ear. "Emma, bring Garrett's lunch to his trailer. His assistant ordered in from Nobu. It's waiting at craft services." Oh, so Garrett didn't just eat in his trailer, he ate different food from the rest of us in his trailer. How nice for him.

Now that I'd been away from the Garrett Glow for a few hours, the effects were wearing off, and I was tired and hungry enough to be a little annoyed that he couldn't get his own damn lunch. I picked up the bags from the same smirking guy at craft services and walked to Garrett's trailer to knock on his door.

I heard his voice inside, talking. Oh good, he was already in there with someone. Maybe it was his assistant, and I could hand lunch to Garrett's minion and leave. The door opened and Garrett was alone, talking into his cell. He smiled, and gestured for me to bring the bags inside. I could handle this, I said to myself. I'm a grown woman and this is my job. I climbed into the trailer, brought the bags to the table, then unpacked two bento boxes and a thermos. I heard him finishing his call.

"So, you're Emma, right?"

I turned and smiled. "That's me! Okay, well, if you need anything else, let me know. Enjoy your lunch!" Even I could tell my voice was weirdly bright and chipper. I headed to the door.

"Hold on a second," Garrett said. "Aren't you hungry? There's plenty of food, why don't you join me?"

"I really shouldn't. But thanks."

Garrett must be a really good actor, I thought, because he looked genuinely disappointed that I was leaving. "I'm sorry, I'm being selfish. You're working like a dog out there and they've probably got you on a short leash. You'd get in all kinds of trouble taking a lunch break on your first day. I know how it is. Listen, some other time, all right?" Then he opened the door for me.

That was it? He wasn't going to try a little harder to get me to stay? I don't know if I looked as surprised as I felt, but Garrett seemed amused as he closed the door behind me. And strangely, I felt just a tiny bit disappointed.

As I walked away, I saw Jen. She looked behind me at Garrett's trailer. "How'd that go?"

"Honestly, it was fine. I gave him his lunch and that was it."

She looked surprised. "Really? He didn't ask you to stay?"

"Oh, well, yeah. He asked. But I said I couldn't, and that was it. I think he just wanted his lunch."

Jen rolled her eyes. "Sure. Come on, let's get some food. They've got roast pork today and I hear it's good."

The pork was a far cry from my grandma's moist and delicious pork shoulder. I nearly snapped the plastic knife in half trying to cut through it. It didn't matter, though. I couldn't have eaten anyway. My nerves were popping, waiting for the next command to be barked in my ear.

By the time I trudged out of the subway, it was after midnight. Even my skin was tired. All day I'd run around the set for coffee, script changes, more coffee, more script changes. After lunch, Stacy put me on crowd control with Jen, and it was insane. For every crazed fan, there was another irritated local who just wanted to walk down the street. And it was our

job to prevent them from doing that. Jen told me I was being
way too polite and no one would take me seriously that way.
After about an hour of trying to be bossy and unsympathetic,
I was relieved when Stacy chirped back in my ear, telling me
that Garrett wanted another iced coffee. I couldn't even look
at Jen.

She needn't have worried about me having any face time
with Garrett, because the set was a clanging machine after
lunch. As the day wore on, Lynch's mood frayed, and that
seemed to shred everyone's nerves from the producers to the
lowliest PAs. And then it started to rain. My phone buzzed and
I saw I had a text from Sam.

See you tonight?

I fought off the urge to dance in the street. Then I looked
at my watch. It was already 9 p.m. and there was no sign we
were stopping anytime soon. I texted back.

I wish, but I'm working. First day, wanna impress. Tomorrow???

Within seconds he replied.

That was all, but it was enough to float me through the
rest of the evening, even if I was damp and chilled and every
bone in my body ached as I unlocked the door to my building that night. As I stepped out of the elevator, I hesitated
for a moment. Would it be too weird to knock on Sam's door
after midnight? Yes. Don't be stupid, Emma. Still, I looked

longingly down the hall toward his apartment. Then I heard his locks click, and my heart caught. The door opened and a blonde with disheveled hair appeared. Then I saw Sam's profile. Maybe she was a friend? Then he bit her ear. Not a friend. I thought I was going to be sick. I turned quickly toward my apartment and fumbled with my keys. I heard music and laughter through the door. Oh God, no. Not one of Lily's impromptu parties.

The party was just Lily and Mikey and a bottle of wine. The cause of the celebration seemed to have something to do with a floral explosion in the center of the room. We didn't have the largest living room, but it wasn't the smallest, either, and yet Lily had to slide across the sofa to get around the massive arrangement of flowers on our coffee table. She was glowing with excitement, and I could only imagine she'd received them from some rich guy she'd met at a club last night. This kind of stuff happened to her all the time. Although these flowers were a little much even by her standards.

"Oh my God, Emma!" Lily launched herself at me, throwing her arms around my neck. I fell backward into the doorknob and yelped.

"Lily, sweetie, I'm kind of tired and I think I just cracked a rib."

Then Mikey flew forward. "Emms, tell us everything!"

I had such incredibly sweet friends. They knew how much this job meant to me, and they had stayed here waiting for me, just so I could tell them about my day. Despite the Sam-shaped rock of disappointment I'd swallowed in the hallway just now, I laughed while I peeled Lily off me. "I'll tell you everything, but let me get these wet clothes off."

Mikey shook his hands spastically. "Hurry up, hurry up. Lily called me the second the flowers arrived and we've been on pins ever since."

Lily held out her hand. "I kind of opened the card."

Wait. What were they talking about? I took the card.

Dear Emma,

Sorry I scared you today. First days are tough. Let's celebrate your new job at dinner tomorrow. I'll send a car for you.

Garrett

"Squee!" That was Mikey.

"Emms, I don't know how you did it, but I *want* to know how you did it." That was Lily.

This was crazy. Yesterday I was a loser college failure, today I was on the set of a Hollywood blockbuster, and now this. I dropped down on the sofa.

"Emma, honey, are you okay? You don't look so hot." Mikey put a hand on my forehead.

"What the hell am I going to do? I can't go out with him. What will everyone on the set think of me? But if I say no, will he get me fired?" I thought about Stacy and Jen. I thought about a big *V* for victim on my forehead.

"Emma, calm yourself." Lily plopped down next to me on the sofa. "Look, I've heard the stories about stars and PAs, but you need to relax. Garrett Walker asked you out. This is a good thing."

"It is?" I wasn't so sure.

Mikey was losing patience. "Come on, honey, he's gorgeous. He's rich. He wants to send a car for you. This is like a movie, I can't even stand it."

"But they told me I shouldn't even go in his trailer," I said.

"And why did they say that?" Lily said. "Because they didn't want you going in his trailer and coming out fifteen minutes later with your hair a mess. But that is not what we're talking about here. Emma, the guy asked you out. On a date. You have been asked out on a date by Garrett Walker." Then she laughed.

And then I laughed, and pretty soon we were all laughing so hard that tears were running down our faces. When we'd settled down enough to talk, I said, "I slept with Sam last night." Lily gasped, and I told them the rest. "I thought he really liked me, but then I saw a girl coming out of his apartment just now. So . . ."

"So he's a dog, Emms." Mikey reached over, pulled a gardenia out of the massive bouquet on the table, and stuck it in my hair. "Now let's move on to more important things . . . like Garrett Walker. I need a play-by-play—no detail is too small, so don't leave anything out."

## 4

I was worried that I'd feel awkward around Garrett the next day, but once I got to the set I realized how ridiculous that was. There wasn't time to breathe, much less flirt—or try not to.

When I saw Dave hustle to craft services and run to Garrett's trailer with a cappuccino in hand, I felt a pang in my stomach. As much as I wanted to avoid Garrett, or at least *thought* I wanted to avoid him, I was disappointed that he hadn't asked for me all morning. Mikey and Lily had gotten me so wound up the night before that I'd really believed I could go out on a date with him, and that it might even be fun. But that was momentary weakness. Back on set, I gave myself a hard shake and remembered that my job was the most important thing. I had no business flirting with Garrett Walker, and I definitely had no business going out with him.

And then, just a few minutes after noon, I heard Stacy's voice in my ear. "Emma, please bring Garrett his lunch."

Shit.

I scurried to craft services and retrieved his lunch (today it was from Babbo; this guy had good taste in food . . .). I tried to mentally compose myself on the walk to his trailer. I'd just drop off the bag and go. No chitchat. Be professional, Emma. You are not that kind of girl.

As I put my hand up to knock on his door, he swung it open. "Hi," he said, cocking his head to one side and smiling, those big brown eyes staring down at me.

Without responding, I held out the bag for him to take it.

"Would you like to come in?" he asked.

"I should really get to lunch," I said. "I don't have much time."

"Two minutes."

"I have to get Mark Lynch his lunch," I lied.

"Did you get the flowers?" he asked.

I nodded and looked down.

"And the note?"

"Yes, I'm sorry," I stammered. "I can't. I'm sorry."

He shrugged, again looking genuinely disappointed, and closed the door. I was trembling and I felt hot tears well up in my eyes. Deep breath.

Garrett was done for the day before I was, and I was put back on crowd control while they filmed some background shots. About 5 p.m., just when I thought a lady was going to hit me with her fake Prada purse, my phone buzzed with a text. It came up "unknown number." Interesting.

Have dinner with me. Just one dinner. Promise I won't bite.—GW

I could hear my mother's voice in my head: *If something seems too good to be true, most likely it's going to explode in your face.* Once again I wondered what I was doing. This wasn't me—I didn't go out with movie stars. This was Lily's dream. I wanted to be behind the camera, the unseen person making the movies.

Then I laughed to myself. Who was I kidding? It was one dinner. Once Garrett realized I wasn't going to sleep with him—and I was certain about that—he'd get bored. And all my qualms and worries would be moot. There would be no more dates with movie stars. Before I could change my mind, I quickly replied to Garrett's text.

Fine. But it's not a date, it's just dinner.

Mikey looked at me appraisingly. I'd raced in and out of the shower, and it was now 7 p.m. Garrett's car was picking me up in an hour, and Mikey was concerned.

He shook his head. "One hour, toots? These are not my preferred working conditions."

"Persevere, Michael. Have faith," Lily giggled. Then she flung open the closet doors. "Okay, this calls for my side of the closet."

She started digging and held up one dress after another in front of me. Mikey sat on the bed and dismissed each dress one by one. "Too slutty. Wrong color for her. Too short. Lily, sweetheart, do you own a dress that covers your crotch?"

Lily sniffed. "Emma's taller than I am. They're not that short on me."

"Stop! That's the one." Mikey stood up. "It's perfect."

"Hold this, Emms." I held the dress up to me and looked

down at myself. It was a simple Diane von Furstenberg wrap dress. Classic, but shape-flattering.

Lily stood next to Mikey and they both looked at me. Mikey assessed me with just one word. "Chicness."

I threw the dress on the bed while they debated over shoes. That was the one thing I couldn't steal from Lily's side of the closet, because my feet were a full size larger than hers.

After I'd finished drying my hair I came back in and Mikey handed me some strappy gold sandals I'd worn to a wedding. "Mikey, those are summer sandals. I'll freeze. It's the middle of October."

He just looked at me. I took the sandals and the dress and went in the other room to change. Sure enough, I looked good. When I came out, Lily was holding a glass of white wine. "Drink up. You need to take the edge off."

I sat down, and suddenly I started to shake a little bit. I looked at them. "Am I really doing this?" I took a deep sip. "Am I really, really doing this?"

"Cheers, dears," Mikey said, and we all clinked glasses.

~~~~~

At first I was disappointed when the car arrived and it was only a driver—no Garrett. But then I realized it made things so much easier if I didn't have to make small talk with him in a car. At least in a restaurant you could distract yourself with the menu.

The car pulled up to a small Italian restaurant on Bond Street called Il Buco. As I was led to a dark table in the corner, I heard my heartbeat in my ears. I looked to my left. Was that Denzel Washington? Oh my God, what was I doing here?

Garrett stood, and he flashed me that grin of his. I smiled back, shakily. Then I felt the seat nudged in behind me, which was a good thing, because my knees actually knocked.

Garrett picked up my hand and warmed it in both of his. "Are you okay?"

"No, I'm terrified." Oh my God, had I just said that out loud?

Garrett laughed with such surprised pleasure that I had to laugh, too. "I like honesty. That's good. I don't get enough of that." He poured me a glass of Brunello, and his brown eyes twinkled with mischief. "Now, what do you like to eat?"

And that was the moment when it all changed. Suddenly I wasn't sitting there with Garrett Walker, movie star. I was with an incredibly handsome guy named Garrett . . . on a date. And this guy—I liked him a lot.

He barely glanced at the menu, and when the waiter came to our table, he knowingly ordered the *carciofi alla giudea,* pasta with white truffles, and *bistecca Fiorentina* for two. Then he started asking me questions, and he didn't stop asking me questions until our entrées were cleared. I told him about Kentucky, my friends, I even told him about losing my scholarship. I told him how much I wanted to be a screenwriter. He nodded and laughed in all the right places, and he looked at me with warm sympathy when I told him how I refused to go home a failure. It wasn't until we were ordering dessert that I realized he hadn't once talked about himself.

"What about you, Garrett? Where did you grow up?"

Garrett smiled. "Don't you know everything about me from *People* magazine?"

"No, and even if I did read those articles, I suspect that's not the whole truth, is it?"

He looked at me and his face grew serious. "The truth is that I am having a wonderful time."

I looked at him across the candlelight and I noticed the beginnings of silver along his temples, and then I saw that one side of his mouth curled up a little more than the other. "Your face is lopsided," I said.

He looked at me and sucked in a shocked burst of laughter. "What did you say?"

"Your face is lopsided," I said. "I like it."

"My mom always called me Funny Face. It was her favorite musical. She loved Fred Astaire. And she wanted me to grow up and marry Audrey Hepburn."

"She sounds like a romantic. My mom isn't at all. I guess my dad ruined it for her."

"Oh believe me, my dad was no prince. He was handsome, for sure—the best that industrial Pennsylvania had to offer. My mom always says he swept her off her feet. Unfortunately for Mom, he had what they used to call a roving eye. He broke her heart over and over and over again. But she never gave up. She kept watching her Hollywood musicals and believing in 'happily ever after' long after she'd lost any chance of having it for herself."

"And then she had herself a movie star in you," I said.

Garrett didn't answer me. Dessert came and I wondered if I'd said something wrong. We ate our tiramisu, and I drank more wine, even though I was long past the point of not needing any more to drink. "Garrett, I'm sorry. I didn't mean to sound flip."

He shook his head. "Don't apologize. It's true. On some

level, I wanted to make sure my life was perfect in every way that hers wasn't. And I've tried to do my best for her. She never left my dad. No matter how many times I begged her. But I did have the chance to take her to the Oscars. I think she enjoyed herself, and she doesn't get to do that enough."

"You're a good son. You must make her really happy."

Then Garrett kissed me. I tasted the wine on his lips, and I ran my fingers lightly through his thick hair.

We parted lips and he looked at me. "Tomorrow night?"

~~~~

The next night we went to another restaurant, and he told me all about the town he grew up in, and how there were never enough jobs for the number of people looking for them. He told me about being captain of the football team and president of the student council and star of the school musical and all the while he was thinking, Just get me out of here.

The more we talked, the more I saw in him—there were so many layers beneath his debonair surface. And the more I got to know him, the more I saw his imperfections, and the less intimidated I was. There was a scar near the corner of one of his eyes, and a pockmark on his forehead, right near his hairline. Of course, he was still staggeringly handsome, but suddenly he was only human, like me. He had acne when he was sixteen, and sometimes he missed a spot when he shaved. He even got spinach in his teeth.

Our third night together, he planned to take me out to dinner again. That day on set was grueling, though, and we didn't break until 10 p.m. He texted me.

I'm beat, but I want to see you. Come to my hotel for room service. Please?

I knew what that meant. But oddly, I wasn't nervous. So I knew it'd be okay. Whatever happened, I had my eyes open.

That night, I didn't dress up. Mikey and Lily were already out somewhere, and I was on my own. I decided that if I was going to do this, then it was time to do it on my own terms, and in my own clothes. I put on my nicest underwear and then pulled on my own jeans and my own boots, and wrapped a scarf around my neck. Then I grabbed my peacoat. Somewhere in the world, this was an appropriate outfit for a third date.

He was living in the Empire Suite of the Carlyle. The ride to the twenty-eighth floor seemed too long, until the doors opened. Then I wondered for a moment if I was making a terrible mistake. I walked to his door and knocked.

He opened the door and smiled at me. For one insane minute I thought about closing the door again and running for the elevator. Instead, I stepped into his arms. He slipped his hands under my peacoat and pushed the door closed behind us. Then he ran his hands up my sides and slipped the coat down my arms. He pulled me in close to him and kissed my lips, softly, slowly, as he unhooked the clasp of my bra with a practiced hand. He took my face in his hands and said, "You're not like anybody else."

I felt dizzy. Then I was running my hands up his torso and it was a tornado of clothes—scarf, shirts, jeans. We stumbled upstairs and into the bedroom, and I was so hungry for him

I didn't want to stop. But suddenly Garrett stepped back and looked at me, standing there in my thong and nothing else. He gave me a mischievous smile and said he'd be right back with a gift he had bought me.

He disappeared and then returned with a tan shoe box tied with a ribbon. Inside was a pair of the highest black patent Christian Louboutin pumps I had ever seen. In truth, I had never seen any Christian Louboutin pumps in person, but I assumed these were the highest. He knelt at my feet and slipped on the heels one by one—a perfect fit.

He worked his way back up my body, lingering in between my legs, before taking me by my waist and pulling me in close to him and kissing my lips, softly, slowly. He picked me up and wrapped my legs around his waist and then laid me down on the bed, pulling my thong down around my ankles and over my feet, leaving my high heels on. He was on top, and then I was on top, and I felt drugged, I was so lost in him. At one point he pressed me up against the floor-to-ceiling windows of the bedroom, the glass cooling my hot skin and the skyline of New York to my back as he thrust inside me. This was no after-hours, drunk college boy fumble—I had never felt anything like this before.

I spent the night and woke up early to shower in the impossibly luxurious bathroom. I looked around me in a state of disbelief. It was the size of my apartment, and Garrett Walker was asleep on the other side of that closed door. This was insane. And I was almost late for work. I pulled on my clothes and quietly kissed Garrett goodbye, wondering secretly if this was it for us. I'd given him everything I had. What else could he possibly want from me?

~~~

Once again I was wrong about Garrett. Not only did he send flowers to my apartment with another invitation to dinner, but we saw each other every night after that. I spent more time in his hotel than in my own apartment, and soon I could tell that Lily was moving past her initial enthusiasm, into outright shock and disbelief. It was one thing to have a date with Garrett Walker. It was quite another to be his girlfriend. And with lightning speed, that's exactly what I was becoming.

Then reality set in. The film wrapped, and I could no longer deny that I would have to get a job. I couldn't bear hostessing again. Maybe I could temp while I scrambled for another PA job. Stacy said she'd keep me in mind, but I had been a last-minute fill-in—there were so many more experienced PAs vying for the same jobs. Once again I felt alone with my anxiety. Lily just shrugged when the word *job* was mentioned in her presence. Mikey worked incredibly hard as an assistant personal shopper at Barneys, but he had a strictly bootstraps mentality—no complaining, just get out there and make something of yourself. And any time I mentioned my concern to Garrett, he just handed me an expensive glass of wine and told me not to worry so much, that life was to be enjoyed.

But I couldn't stop worrying. My mother's pessimism was bred into me, and I couldn't believe that any of this would last. Garrett would move on to another movie, and even his best intentions couldn't overcome the boredom factor. It might have been nice for a while for him to be with a real person who cared for him. But it couldn't last.

Of course, I didn't tell Garrett any of this. But when my mood was too dark to ignore, he surprised me with a trip to the Hamptons. He said winter was his favorite time there. The cold meant it was deserted, and the beach was moody and stormy, just the way he liked it. Mark Lynch had offered Garrett his place in East Hampton, and he promised me it would be beautiful—a sprawling house, right on the ocean, two fireplaces, no staff, and nothing but time to enjoy each other. And if we got bored—unlikely—we agreed that we would watch our favorite movies. Each of us was to bring three of our all-time favorites. And the rule was that we couldn't compare lists in advance. Garrett made me unveil my stack first: He smirked at *Dirty Dancing*, and I told him that it was a work of staggering genius that he must learn to appreciate if he ever wanted to have sex with me again. Then I pulled out *When Harry Met Sally*—I just loved all of Nora Ephron's screenplays. He nodded and shrugged. Last I pulled out *Breakfast at Tiffany's* and gave him a hard look. "I dare you to smirk," I said. Garrett smiled and then reached for his bag. First was *On the Waterfront*. I couldn't argue with that. Next was *Godfather II*. "Figures," I said. Last was . . . *Breakfast at Tiffany's*. We both laughed.

The weekend was everything Garrett promised. I was happy, but it all felt bittersweet, like an end to something. I told him I'd make dinner—country-fried steak, green beans, and mashed potatoes. Chocolate pudding for dessert. I hadn't had to think twice about the menu: It was the same meal I'd been making since I was a kid. When Mom was at work, Grandma let me keep her company in the kitchen, and country-fried steak was the one recipe I'd mastered. And now here I was, worlds away. I thought I'd gotten over the unreality of this life I was leading with Garrett, but the absurdity of it all swept over me once again. This was as close to normal as my life had been in the last few months—sitting on stools at the island in this airy kitchen, lights dimmed, and real food on our plates. But nothing about this was normal.

"Emma, you are the woman of my dreams. I can't even remember the last time anyone cooked for me."

I laughed. "People cook for you all the time, Garrett. You just don't know them."

Garrett looked at me. "You're laughing but you don't sound happy. What's going on, Emma?"

"I'm happy! I'm happier than I've ever been."

*"But . . ."* Garrett looked at me with his big brown eyes. There was no twinkle.

"But I know it's coming to an end," I said. "And it's okay. I'm realistic. I'm just a little sad, that's all." I shrugged.

"Emma, what are you talking about?" He looked sincerely baffled.

"You know. The movie's wrapped. You're moving on. It's okay."

"Emma, you are truly an idiot. Do you think I have ever been with a woman like you before? Do you think I've ever even brought a woman here before? Usually I'm alone and eating frozen pizza when I'm out here. And I love it, because I never get to be alone. But now I want to be alone with you. No one else. Do you know what that means to me?"

I just stared at him until he reached over with an outstretched finger and gently closed my mouth. Then he kissed me on the lips.

I blinked at him and I could feel my eyes filling. Please let me not cry.

Garrett smiled and wiped the corner of one of my eyes. Then he licked his finger. "Emma Guthrie, what are you doing for Christmas?"

## 5

I was in love with Garrett Walker. That was no surprise to me—that feeling had been building over the last month. I should have been happy about it—blissful. But instead the feeling had terrified me. I was in way too deep, and when the end came I'd be devastated. I could hear my mom's voice in my head: *Emma, there are more fish in the sea than anyone ever pulled out of it.* Now, though, after Garrett's reassurance over a plate of country-fried steak (thanks, Grandma), I let the tiniest feeling of security creep in. And that feeling . . . it was wonderful. It suddenly struck me that I had never, not once in my whole life that I could remember, felt truly secure. I'd always believed that my fate rested solely in my slender hands, and that one wrong move would send me back to Kentucky, dreams crushed, working at the strip mall.

Instead I was going to St. Barts for Christmas. Garrett had invited me to spend an entire week with him on a private yacht he had chartered in the Caribbean. I'd never been south of Myrtle Beach, South Carolina, and I had no idea what to expect. But I imagined seven days just like the weekend we'd spent in the Hamptons. Instead of winter weather keeping the crowds away, this time it would be miles and miles of turquoise water as far as the eye could see. And just me and Garrett, alone on a ship in all that blue.

I couldn't wipe the smile off my face the whole evening after Garrett had asked me to go with him, and Garrett looked like a kid, he was so proud of himself for making me happy. "Now that's more like it," he said, laughing. "You're beautiful even when you're sad, but you're much more beautiful when you're happy."

There was just one catch: I always spent Christmas at home in Kentucky, and I told Garrett that it would break my mother's heart if I didn't come home. Garrett wouldn't let me worry about that. "I'll come pick you up the day after Christmas and take you to the airport. And that way I can meet your mom before I whisk away her daughter. Problem solved."

What I didn't tell Garrett, however, was that my family didn't even know about him. The one person I'd told was Grace—I couldn't keep this from her, and I needed someone to share it all with. Lily was becoming harder and harder to confide in, but Grace just listened and reassured. She didn't try to pretend I had nothing to worry about, but she was good at reminding me that no matter what happened I'd be fine—with Garrett or without him. She had a way of making me believe her.

I had confessed to my mother that I'd left school, because it was too hard to dodge her questions about that, and at least I had the PA job to use as an excuse. But Garrett—that was another story. How could I possibly explain *him* to my mother? It had been two months and *I* still wasn't used to the idea. She couldn't begin to understand that her daughter was dating a movie star—even I didn't understand it. I had told myself that the relationship would be over before it was even an issue—there was no sense telling her if Garrett was going to break my heart anyway. And if I told my mother, she'd tell my sister, Maureen, and that I could not bear. Maureen would blab to everyone in town how her little sister had given it up for Garrett Walker and then been kicked to the curb.

I shook myself. That wasn't my story line. Garrett wasn't kicking me to the curb, he was taking me to St. Barts. And it was normal to tell your family about your boyfriend.

This was my internal dialogue—the blissful Emma on one side of the conversation, and the anxious Emma on the other—as Garrett and I flew back from our weekend in East Hampton by chartered helicopter. Manhattan rose beneath us, and anxious Emma seemed to be winning the internal debate as we landed and I placed my foot on solid ground. I felt Garrett's demeanor change the second we stepped out, and I wondered if the same dose of reality was hitting him. I looked at his face and he seemed angry for a split second, and then his face became blank and unreachable. He grabbed my hand and his head of security put his arm around me on the other side. I was confused until I saw what had caused that reaction in Garrett—a pack of photographers with long white camera lenses.

———〰———

"Oh my God, Emma. You're in Page Six." Lily held the paper up to me. "This is huge. They don't know your name, but that's just a matter of time."

Garrett had warned me this was coming. Once he saw the photographers, he said it was inevitable. Ugh. I looked scared stiff in the picture and I was wearing that stupid peacoat.

"So is Garrett pissed?" Lily poked me to get me to pay attention to her.

"Well, he wasn't thrilled to see the photographers."

"Hmm." Lily looked away.

"What, Lily? If there's something on your mind, say it." This was my first day of unemployment, and I hadn't had my second cup of coffee yet, so I was feeling a little testy. After the initial glow of happiness about St. Barts, now I was back to worrying about Christmas with my family.

"It's just that, well . . . you always say that Garrett's a really private guy. I mean, I haven't even met him." She looked at me meaningfully. This had become a sore spot between us, even though I explained to her that Garrett and I never went to parties or even out to dinner with friends: It was always just the two of us. "And I just wonder how he'll feel about you guys being public. That's all." Lily flipped the pages of the paper so she wouldn't have to look at me while she dropped her bomb.

"So you think Garrett's going to dump me out of embarrassment?"

Lily cringed. I guess she wasn't expecting me to be so direct. "Oh, honey, no. I mean that would be terrible." She put her hand on my arm. "What do I know, anyway? It's just that people like Garrett have so much pressure on them and they need to choose their relationships carefully. It's all publicity, you know that."

Wow, Lily really knew how to hit my sensitive spots. Of course, I'd thought the same thing. It was fine for Garrett to see me when his opinion was the only one that mattered. But what would happen when everyone else found out that he was dating an unemployed PA sixteen years younger than him? That wouldn't exactly add luster to his résumé. And while I pretended to Lily that Garrett was past needing to care about whom he dated, I knew: No one in Hollywood was past caring about that.

My cell buzzed with a text. Probably Mikey. I was surprised it took him this long. Page Six was his gospel. I reached across the coffee table and picked up the phone, then tried to suppress my smile of triumph. It was Garrett.

That picture doesn't do you justice. Next time we'll give them a better angle.

I smiled and texted back:

You're not mad?

Not a second passed before he replied:

Nah. It's just the fame tax.

I tucked my phone in the pocket of my hoodie and picked up the rest of the paper.

"Who was it?" Lily asked.

"Grace. Making plans for Christmas."

"God. Are you as bummed as I am? Christmas in New Jersey for me. Woo-hoo." Lily twirled a finger in the air.

"Well, I'm not looking forward to seeing holier-than-thou sister Maureen. But I love seeing my mom and grandparents. It's just that Mom gives me that concerned face. She has this way of looking at me like she's afraid my head's going to pop off. And now I have to break the news to her about Garrett."

Lily looked at me. "Really? You think that's a good idea? I mean, why even go there? Won't they just worry?"

I sighed. "I have to tell them, because I'm leaving the day after Christmas to go to St. Barts. With Garrett."

Lily's eyebrows shot up at the same time her chin dropped.

"Be happy for me, Lily. Okay?"

"Oh, honey, of course I am!" She quickly recomposed her face. "That's amazing!"

I smiled at her. "It is, isn't it?"

~~~~~

Mikey dropped at least ten party dresses in a pile on the bed. "You have to take these. Lily and I discussed it, and this is an investment in the future. She's happy to have you borrow them. Aren't you, Lily?"

"Absolutely!" Lily said, a little too brightly.

I looked at the pile of dresses. "Guys, you're nuts. I have one bag, I'm going to Kentucky first, and I have to pack all my family's Christmas presents. And then I'm going on a beach vacation with Garrett. I've got room for bikinis, shorts, and flip-flops. That's it."

Mikey put his hand on his chest in mock horror. "Emms,

no, no. You are going to St. Barts and you're going to be on a yacht. A yacht. This isn't a rowboat on the Mississippi, sweetheart."

I laughed. "Thank you for your concern, but I'll be fine. I promise."

"That's right, Mikey," Lily chimed in. "Don't worry about her. She won't be wearing any clothes, anyway. Right, Emms?"

I threw a spangly dress at her. "Seriously guys, you're both very sweet. I wish I could take you with me."

Mikey shook his head. "That's really shameful, Emma. You don't mean a word you just said. And I couldn't be more proud of you."

My grandparents' dinner table groaned with food. Baked ham, scalloped potatoes, homemade yeast rolls, deviled eggs. And on the counter in the kitchen were three kinds of pies— pumpkin, chess, and lemon meringue. Grandma's cooking was just too good to pass up—I'd stuffed my face well beyond what I should have, to the point that I'd had to undo the top button of my jeans. I'd be paying for my sins tomorrow when I had to put on a bikini.

My whole family was sitting in my grandparents' living room sipping iced sweet tea and opening presents. Maureen's three kids, ages two, four, and five, were tearing through wrapping paper, squealing with delight at the toys, and tossing the books behind them. Then the oldest, Stella, came up to sit next to me.

"Hey, Stella, why don't you go get my present to you from under the tree. It's right over there." Stella ran over to get it and ripped through the wrapping. Inside was a fleece-lined jacket with "Rough Justice" embroidered on the back. "That's the name of the movie I worked on, honey."

"Cool, Aunt Emma!" Stella stood up and put on the jacket. It fell to her toes.

"It's a little big," Maureen said, blandly. Leave it to Maureen to state the obvious—as long as it was negative. Her stupid husband, Glenn, just snickered.

"The star of the movie, Garrett Walker, had those made for everyone who worked on the movie. I got one for each of the kids. They're keepsakes. I didn't expect they'd be able to wear them now." I looked at Maureen, then smiled back at Stella. "Look in the pocket, honey."

Stella pulled a piece of paper from the pocket, and her face wrinkled in confusion.

My mother stood up to reach for the paper and read it out loud. "Dear Stella, I hope you like the jacket. I'm looking forward to meeting you. Love, Garrett Walker."

Granddad said, "Well, I'll be darned."

I felt heat rising to my cheeks, and I knew this was the moment. If I didn't tell them now they'd only be angry at me later for keeping it from them.

Grandma said, "Well, isn't that just the sweetest thing. Stella, he was in that movie we saw in the summer. The one with all the cars crashing together. You remember that one, honey?"

"Hmph." That was Maureen.

"Is there something wrong, Maureen?" I asked. Why do I always rise to her bait?

"Just seems to me he shouldn't have made a promise he couldn't keep, is all." Maureen looked at her nails, as if trying to find a chip in the polish. "Unless Garrett Walker's stopping by for Christmas dinner." Glenn guffawed in response.

Mom tried to make nice. "Well, Maureen, I'm sure he didn't mean any harm. It's just something nice you say to a child. He doesn't have any kids of his own. He couldn't know how they latch on to things."

"Well, actually, Mom, the thing is . . . Garrett and I are friends."

"Well, that's lovely, honey," Mom said uneasily, and looked at me with that concerned expression on her face. Maureen watched us like a turkey vulture ready to pounce on roadkill.

"We're kind of more than friends, Mom." I glanced around the room quickly and then back at my mother. "Garrett's my boyfriend."

Granddad said, "Well, I'll be darned."

Grandma said, "Oh my."

Mom looked at me like my head was about to pop off. "Your boyfriend? You mean . . . you're dating Garrett Walker?"

I glanced quickly at Maureen and Glenn. Maureen looked momentarily confused, like even she couldn't come up with a nasty thing to say. Glenn looked at her uncertainly. If Maureen didn't have a reaction, he was lost as to what to say or do himself.

"For a few months now, Mom. I would have told you sooner, but I wanted to wait until I was sure it was serious."

Mom looked at me, a frightened expression on her face. "And it's serious?"

I nodded. "He's invited me to go on vacation with him to the Caribbean. And I accepted. And he's picking me up here . . . tomorrow."

My mother's response was immediate and dramatic. She

turned white as a ghost and sank into the recliner she had been standing in front of, shaking her head.

I sat on the arm of the chair, gently hugged her shoulders, and then took her hand. "Mom, I'm sorry. I know you'll miss me, but it's only a week and I'll come back really soon. I promise."

Mom shook her head, and her words were hard to understand. "Now I . . . now I . . . now I . . ."

"Cheryl, honey," Grandma said to my mother. "Calm yourself now. Emma's gonna be fine and she'll be back real soon. Won't you, honey?" She looked at me encouragingly.

Maureen sucked her teeth in disgust.

"Of course I will, Mom, and until I get a new job, I'll have all kinds of time."

Finally, Mom pulled herself together and patted my hand. Granddad handed her a tissue and she blew her nose fiercely. "Oh, precious, it's not that. I mean, I'll miss you and all, and I haven't even begun to wrap my head around the thought of my baby girl dating a celebrity, for heaven's sake." She looked around the living room in despair. "It's just that now I'm gonna have to clean this whole damn house."

Granddad chuckled, and Grandma patted my mother's hand in sympathy.

Poor Mom. She wasn't as worried about me leaving with Garrett as she was about Garrett coming here, and what he'd think of the house. "Mom, how about you take me to the airport tomorrow, and you can meet Garrett there? Would that be better?"

Mom sniffed and her face brightened with relief. "Oh yes, honey. That's much better."

⌇⌇⌇

That night, I was sorting through my suitcase in my old childhood room when there was a soft knock on the door.

Mom stepped in and smiled at me. "Can I help you, honey? Need me to do any laundry for you before you leave?"

"I'm good, Mom."

"All right, honey. Well, you just let me know if there's anything I can do." She was nervously standing in the doorway, as if she were undecided on stepping forward or back.

"Mom, I know I should have told you sooner about Garrett and I'm sorry."

She looked at me and tied and then retied her robe. Then she came and sat down on my old twin bed with its faded quilt and stuffed animals that she'd never had the heart to throw away. "Sweetheart, are you taking care of yourself? I mean . . . are you . . . protected?"

Oh good God, please tell me my mother wasn't going to ask me about birth control. I must have looked as stricken as I felt because she quickly added, "Heavens, I don't mean that." She blushed to the roots of her hair, and I felt the heat rise to my own cheeks. Then she said, "No, honey, I mean, he's older than you are, and he's from a different world than we are. And well, he's not like us, is he?"

She wasn't wrong. Garrett was definitely not like us. And I'd had the same exact conversation in my own head at least a million times since my first date with him, so I could hardly blame my mother for voicing it. "Well, he's not that old, Mom. He's only thirty-eight. And he's a really kind, sweet man. He wasn't always a movie star, and his family never had any money growing up. We have a lot more in common than you might think." I sounded more defensive than I'd wanted to, and my mother patted my knee and her face was serious and attentive.

"Fair enough, honey. I don't know him, and you do. You know I just want you to be safe and happy. Are you happy?"

I hugged her and caught the familiar scent of her drugstore shampoo, the same brand she'd been using for as long as I could remember. My eyes got a little wet with the memories that flooded back—it was the same scent I'd breathed when I was a little girl and my mother kissed me goodbye early in the morning when she went to work, and then kissed me good night again when she came home after a double shift. "I am, Mom. I really am."

## 6

"Good morning," Garrett whispered in my ear as he softly brushed the hair from my face. "How'd you sleep?"

It took me a second to realize where I was. "So well," I said through a yawn. "I think I've recovered from the flight. You didn't prep me for that one, Mr. Action Hero. That's as close to a stunt as I'll ever get."

Garrett had conveniently neglected to tell me that the flight into St. Barts is infamously terrifying for the faint of heart. After landing in St. Maarten, you have the choice of a long, stomach-rocking ferry or a ten-minute flight. Garrett chose the latter, and it was the most terrifying ten minutes of my life. The plane was tiny, with only enough room for us, our bags, and the pilot, but it wasn't the flight itself that was so scary—it was the landing that had me white-knuckling Garrett's arm. The tiny prop plane came up over a mountain, then the pilot *turned off the engine* and dropped directly down onto the runway, braking like crazy so as not to slide right into St. Jean's Bay.

"I promise you'll be happy you made the trip, my dear," he said sweetly, pulling me close to him to spoon.

"I already am."

And I was. After the pent-up anxiety of Christmas, I was ready to enjoy all of this. All I wanted was to have a lazy romantic vacation with Garrett. Sun and sex were the only two things on my agenda.

Speaking of sex . . . a little morning action never hurt anybody, and by the pressure in the small of my back I could tell that Garrett was thinking the same thing. I rolled over and kissed him deeply, then turned him on his back and climbed on top of him.

~~~~~

An hour later I woke up and stretched luxuriously. This was just what I needed. I thought back on the day before. It was bizarre from beginning to end. Mom and my grandparents drove with me to the airport in one car, and Maureen, Glenn, and the kids followed behind. I would vastly have preferred to leave them at home, but after the big deal Maureen had made over Garrett's promise to Stella, there was no way I could. I was so nervous it would be awkward, hoping no one would act weird around him. I just wanted it to be normal—like they were meeting a "regular" guy who was my boyfriend. But then again, how "normal" was it to meet your daughter's boyfriend at the airport just before she boards his private jet? For the whole trip to the airport my stomach was in knots.

In the end, it was uneventful. Garrett met us in a private waiting room, and he took me in his arms to say hello so gently and naturally that no one showed the slightest sign of discomfort. He kissed my mother and grandmother on the cheek, and shook Granddad's and Glenn's hands with manly vigor. Then he embraced Maureen like his own long-lost sister, and she blushed five shades of red. He gave each of the kids a Yankees ball cap, and within minutes they were swinging from his arms. Why was I surprised? Garrett always knew how to charm a room.

When my family left, a car drove us from the private waiting room exit right to the steps of the airplane, a G5. As soon as we were on board, a flight attendant brought us drinks. Once in the air we lounged on a plush couch under cashmere blankets watching movies, and we ate lunch—catered by Mario Batali at Garrett's request—at a dining table. When we landed in St. Maarten, we didn't have to go inside the airport—customs checked our passports right on the plane and then took us in a van across the tarmac to our St. Barts puddle jumper.

That evening when we arrived on the yacht, we were met by a staff of ten—a combination of Australians and South Africans wearing white polo shirts and navy shorts. They all greeted me as Ms. Guthrie and we were handed chilled wet washcloths and fruit smoothies the second we set foot on the boat. The sun had set by then and after a lovely meal of fresh fish and champagne, I collapsed into bed. We weren't as alone as I'd thought we'd be, but I guess I should have known. After all, someone had to drive the boat, right?

I'd wanted to give Garrett his Christmas present the night before, but the moment never seemed right. I dug into my suitcase and pulled out the package that I'd wrapped in white paper and gold ribbon.

When I made it upstairs to the main deck, Garrett was climbing out of the water and back onto the boat. As he toweled himself dry, the sunlight was glistening off the water, creating a glow on his skin that would have taken a lighting director hours to replicate. One look and there was no doubt in my mind why women turned to putty at the sight of him. I couldn't believe I ever thought I could resist him.

"Well hello, sleepy head," he said, flashing a big grin.

"I didn't feel like getting dressed quite yet," I said, tilting my chin down at my cotton robe. Then I looked back at him and raised my eyebrows. "How's the water?"

"It's amazing, Emma. You have to jump in. I'll go back in with you."

"Are you kidding?" I said. "You mean, jump off the side of the boat, right into the ocean?" My fingers involuntarily tightened around the package I held, just at the thought of going in the water.

Garrett laughed. "That's the idea, Emma. That's what people do in the Caribbean. They swim in the ocean."

"But it's so deep." I gingerly edged toward the side of the boat and looked down. "You can't even see the bottom. There could be sharks!"

Garrett put his arms around me. "I'll protect you," he said.

"Great. You can protect me right here. Because I'm not going in there. No way."

He pulled away and smiled at me, then gave me a kiss. "Okay, baby, I got it. No ocean swims for you."

"Anyway, I couldn't wait to give you this." I held out the package to him and his face lit up like a Christmas tree.

"I love presents. Gimme." Garrett tugged the package away from me and ripped at it with all the gusto of my five-year-old niece.

Inside was a shadow box frame with a picture we'd taken of the two of us in the Hamptons one evening, when I'd insisted on walking on the beach even though it was freezing cold. I'd held out the camera in front of our smiling faces and we looked like any happy couple on the beach, which is what I liked about it. Inside I'd glued a few of the shells we'd picked up that day. "Do you like it?"

"Emma, it's beautiful. I love it. It's the nicest thing anyone's ever given me."

"Stop," I said, laughing.

"No, I mean it. No one's ever made me anything before. It's perfect. You're perfect." And he kissed me. When we parted he was holding a small black velvet box in his hand. "Merry Christmas."

My hands shook a little when I flipped open the box. Nestled inside were two perfect diamond studs. They sparkled with fire in the sun and I gasped with pleasure. "Oh my God, Garrett. I love them!"

"Really?" He grinned like a kid who'd gotten his first hit in baseball. "I didn't think you had anything like that. And they reminded me of you. Beautiful—and classic."

I put them in my ears right away. "I am never, ever taking them off."

"Good." Garrett smiled and kissed me again. "Now let's eat. I was waiting for you and I'm starving."

We sat down to a gorgeous breakfast of fresh fruit and

pastries. The freshly baked croissants were still warm from the oven and the creamy European-style butter melted on contact—heavenly. And just when I thought this vacation couldn't get any more perfect, I heard the buzz of a dinghy approaching our boat. I expected it to keep buzzing by, but then it stopped, and within seconds a stunning redhead dressed in a hot pink caftan pulled up to the landing of the boat and hopped on.

I was startled, and shrank into my robe, wondering for a moment if this might be a crazed fan looking for her moment with Garrett.

Judging by Garrett's face, though, he knew her, and he looked happy to see her. In fact, he jumped up from the table. Please tell me she wasn't an ex-girlfriend.

"Garrett Walker!" she said, drawing out his name. "You didn't tell me you were coming to St. Barts for New Year's! You should have stayed with us!"

"And be your token celebrity?" he said teasingly, as he folded her in his arms.

I was suddenly desperate to toss myself off the boat. Here was this gorgeous, sophisticated woman, dressed to the nines, her hair blowing perfectly in the breeze, and then there was me—in a gray jersey bathrobe with bed head. It was like my first day of college all over again. Funny how you can go from feeling on top of the world to feeling like some dumb hick in a matter of minutes. I slid out of my seat at the table and toward the cabin, hoping I could slip back inside unnoticed. No such luck.

"Riley, I'd like you to meet my girlfriend, Emma," Garrett said turning to me.

"Hi there," Riley said with a warm smile as she stretched

out her hand. "It's so nice to meet you. I'm sorry if I interrupted your breakfast."

"Oh, no worries," I said, trying my best to pull myself together. "Nice to meet you as well."

"You know what it's like here," she said. "Especially this time of year, manners get tossed to the wind and no one thinks twice about dropping in uninvited." She glanced out toward the water. "It looks like the harbor really filled up overnight. Let the parties begin!"

I looked out over the side of the boat toward the island, and sure enough, it was like a campground of giant yachts.

"Are those all cruise ships?" I asked.

Riley gave me a puzzled expression. "Is this your first time to St. Barts?" she asked.

"Yes, this is all new to me," I said, suddenly realizing I'd asked a stupid question.

"Oh, that explains it," she said. "Nope, no cruise ships, these are all private yachts. The week between Christmas and New Year's here is crazy. Everyone is here. That boat over there is Barry Diller's, that's Rupert Murdoch's over there, that one is Ronald Perelman's, that one belongs to David Geffen and Larry Ellison, that's Paul Allen's . . . " It was like a game of Battleship . . . billionaire edition.

Riley continued to rattle off names, while I nodded blankly, trying to process all the ways in which this vacation was completely different than I'd imagined. Riley must have sensed that I was feeling like a deer in the headlights.

"I'll tell you what," she said to me. "I'm having a few girls over for lunch today: You should join us. Garrett, I'm sure you can find something else to do for a few hours."

Her invitation sounded more like a statement than a question—so much for a quiet, romantic day with Garrett.

"One o'clock, on my boat," she said before I could get an answer out. "See you then." And just as fast as she had appeared, she was gone.

"Um, who was that?" I asked Garrett.

"That's Riley Schwartz," he said. "She's married to Ian Schwartz. He owns practically every building in Manhattan. You'll love Riley, she's tons of fun." Garrett seemed absentminded and unfocused all of a sudden, so different from the way he was this morning. "Riley knows every party, every restaurant, every place to shop—you name it."

"Oh, okay, great," I said, trying not to sound disappointed. I had to be an adult about this. I had no interest in going to lunch with Riley and her rich girlfriends, but if that's what I had to do to be polite, then that's what I'd do. I should be happy about this. I had yet to meet any of Garrett's friends, so this was a huge step for us. He obviously really liked Riley, and this was my chance to get to know her.

"This works out well, actually," Garrett said. "Now I can have lunch with Ari."

"Your agent is here?"

"Of course," he said. "Everybody comes to St. Barts for New Year's."

Right, of course. Silly me. How could I have forgotten?

The captain of our boat made arrangements with the captain of Riley's boat to drop me off in the dinghy for lunch. Getting dressed was a nightmare—clearly I should have listened to Mikey about what to pack. Although that stack of spangly party dresses wasn't going to help me now; even Lily didn't keep a stash of caftans in her closet. The best I could do was a white button-down with the sleeves rolled up, cutoff jean shorts, and sunglasses. Shoes, thank God, were not an issue. Apparently no one wears shoes on yachts. Let's hope my diamond studs would distract from the rest of my outfit.

We pulled up to the Schwartzes' boat and there was an attendant waiting with a tray of cold towels. This was similar to the greeting at our arrival yesterday, but then I had assumed it was a nice gesture after our long journey. I guess it was another yacht thing. Yacht Purell. "Good afternoon, Ms. Guthrie," the attendant said, while using silver tongs to pass me a towel. "The ladies are by the pool. Just go up these stairs to the second level."

A pool? On a boat? Timidly, I walked up and stood at the top of the stairs for a second before going all the way, peering around the corner to assess the situation.

"Emma, welcome!" Riley said with enthusiasm. "Come join us!"

There were four other women, all in their thirties and forties, all looking fabulous. Two were in bikinis, both with taut and toned bodies and perky round breasts. One looked like she was probably a model, tall and thin with a pixie haircut and wearing a sheer black wrap. Another wore a white embroidered tunic and had long, curly blond hair topped with a big straw hat. Then there was Riley, in a different caftan than this morning, and looking, if possible, even more radiant. The scene was like a living, breathing Michael Kors ad.

And then there was me. I looked like a cute college student on spring break, at best.

I walked over to the side of the pool and sat down, putting my legs into the water. Within seconds another attendant was filling a glass of vintage Dom Perignon for me, and yet another

member of the staff brought me a plush Hermès beach towel
and asked if I needed any sunblock.

Riley made all the necessary introductions, but I was so
overwhelmed I couldn't remember everyone's names. I did
recognize one of the last names, belonging to the blonde, who
must have been the wife of a studio head. Her husband had
visited the set of Garrett's movie one day and I had never seen
the set so tense. Mark Lynch even tucked in his shirt.

Lunch was served shortly after I arrived. The chef had
set up a buffet that would have been luxurious even for a
wedding back home. There was caviar, lobster, all sorts of
salads, freshly baked breads, and the expensive champagne
and rosé kept flowing. I noticed I was the only one who took
any pasta salad or bread. I was also the only one that got up
for seconds. Now I was gathering the secret to their taut,
toned bodies.

They weren't unfriendly. In fact, they were all unfailingly
polite. But Riley was the only one who generated any real
warmth. I got the distinct feeling that none of the women
really cared to get to know me. They mostly compared notes
on exercise and which workouts yielded the best results. Then
the conversation shifted to a lot of talk about the party lineup
for the week, and my heart sank. There was an event every
night, and it finally dawned on me that this was not going to
be a vacation alone with Garrett. This was going to be a series
of see-and-be-seen parties. It was a business trip for him—one
that I'd tagged along on unwittingly.

The blonde started talking about which celebrities were
staying on which billionaires' boats, and that seemed to
spark the most excitement of any topic of conversation so far.
Apparently Paul Allen had Beyoncé and Jay-Z—he'd actu-

ally had a recording studio built in his yacht just to attract the biggest names in music, as if his yacht weren't enough of a draw. Someone else had Bono, and then it was all first names after that—Penelope, Bruce, Jennifer. I thought about Garrett, and what he'd said to Riley about being her token celebrity—but listening to these ladies made me realize that these celebrities weren't tokens, they were trophies. Being rich and powerful wasn't enough for these people. They all wanted to bask in the glow of the truly famous. The women kept on talking around me, seemingly unaware—or unconcerned—that I was there with one of those famous trophies. Which suited me just fine. The last thing I wanted was to be put on the spot; I was content just to recede into the background.

I had nothing to add to the conversation anyway. But then I started to worry that they'd find me aloof if I didn't contribute, and I didn't want Riley to think I was rude. When there was a momentary lull, I asked, "So what kind of work do you guys do?"

It was like a scene in a movie: Someone does something beyond embarrassing; the DJ suddenly cuts off the music, and everyone turns and looks.

The studio-head wife looked at me and said, *"Work?"* as if I'd just uttered an ugly four-letter word. "Why would I want to *work?"*

Then they all laughed and went back to talking about the party everyone was going to that night. I went back to silently counting the minutes until I could leave.

Right after the first woman said her goodbyes, I figured I was in the clear and I asked Riley if her captain could call to have the dinghy brought back for me.

"Actually," she said, "why don't you stick around for a little while after everyone has left?"

"Lovely!" I smiled brightly. Lord, help me.

~~~

Once the last of the ladies had boarded her dinghy (or "tender," as a few of them called it), Riley offered to give me a tour of her boat. It was at least twice the size of the one Garrett had chartered, and the living room was gorgeous, with clean lines and enormous windows to let in light and views. Then she took me to her massive stateroom, which had a walk-in closet practically the size of the house I grew up in. Inside the closet were more closets, all glass-encased and lit from within—and filled with enough designer clothing to outfit a Madison Avenue showroom.

"Wow," I said. "I really did underpack. How many suitcases did you have to bring?"

"None," she said. "That's the great thing about having a boat. I keep a whole wardrobe here so I never have to pack for vacation. And of course, anything I don't have I can get in town."

Oh. Of course.

Riley took my hand and led me out of the closet. Then she sat on the bed and patted the spot next to her like I was a little girl and she was about to braid my hair. I'd been subjected to enough condescension for one day and was beginning to resent being treated like the child I felt like on the inside. Still, Riley really seemed to be trying to welcome me, so it made me feel even more the petulant child to be offended. I sat down next to her, a few hand-spans away from where she'd directed me.

"Listen, Emma, I know what you're going through. I wasn't always Mrs. Schwartz of Park Avenue, London, and Beverly Hills. I used to be Riley Daniels of Milwaukee, Wisconsin." She smiled at the surprise on my face. "What, you thought I was to the manor born?" She shook her head. "Almost no one you'll meet this week was born this way. They all started somewhere else, and they ended up here, whether by making money or marrying money. And a lot of them want to forget where they came from, because that's not who they are anymore, and they never want to be that way again."

"I can understand that," I said. I thought about my mother's living room, full of Christmas knickknacks and gently worn furniture, and how horrified she was at the thought that Garrett would see it. Even though Garrett's family home was probably no different.

Riley smiled at me. "Honey, you look terrified. And with good reason. This is a whole new world for you. Garrett should have prepared you. No surprise—he's such a typical man that way. That's why I made sure to get you alone today—everyone needs a big sister when they first get thrown into this world."

I started to protest, but Riley held up a hand. "I love Garrett, not to worry. But he should have known what he was dragging you into and given you a little warning. Luckily, I know just how to pay him back. We're going shopping with his credit card. I'll give you an outfit to wear now, and we'll spend the rest of the afternoon in Gustavia. It will be fun. My friends are so used to spending money they don't even think twice about it anymore. It will be nice to shop with someone who can still get excited. Like a virgin." She laughed.

"Oh no," I said. "I couldn't use Garrett's credit card. I wouldn't feel right."

"Emma, Garrett is a rich man. And it will make him feel good to take care of you and buy you nice things. Trust me." She grabbed her cell phone and texted Garrett.

Shame on you! Emma has nothing to wear. I'm sending the tender for your credit card . . . I'm taking her shopping!

Riley wouldn't take no for an answer, and at this point I wasn't going to put up much more of a fight. My suitcase was filled with T-shirts, flip-flops, and swimsuits, and clearly I was in need of a more fashionable wardrobe if I was going to survive this vacation.

The rest of the afternoon was a haze of designer merchandise—Calypso, Hermès, Ralph Lauren, we hit them all. Dresses, jewelry, jeans, shoes, tops, skirts—Riley piled them into my dressing room. The final tally of the bill? Twelve thousand dollars. I nearly choked. That was more than my rent for a year.

Riley gave me a knowing look. "Once you pop your cherry, you'll be surprised how quickly you get used to it."

Garrett was standing with his back to me, looking over the railing at the sun setting over the sea. I snuck up behind him and nibbled on his ear.

I could feel him smile against my cheek, and then he turned to face me. "You look . . . beautiful. More gorgeous than I've ever seen you. And it's not the dress, or the light. It's something else."

"Oh no, I'm pretty sure it's the dress," I said.

I was wearing a long cream silk Lanvin dress and the diamond earrings he'd given me that I refused to take off, and I had pinned my hair into a side knot with a flower. Garrett tucked a strand of hair behind my ear. "It's not just the dress, Emma. You're glowing like that Caribbean sun out there."

"I guess I'm just happy." I ran my fingers through his hair and along the sharp outline of his cheek and jaw. It was our last night in St. Barts. It wasn't the quiet, romantic trip I'd envisioned, and I couldn't say that I would ever get used to the rounds of parties and the constant flow of visitors. But I'd been with Garrett almost every minute of every day, and that I had loved. We had our own little vacation routine: wake up, make love (usually nice, slow sex in the morning), share breakfast and coffee, take a beach walk, lunch on someone's boat or at Taiwana (the first time we went there I nearly choked when I saw the prices—grilled fish and a salad ran around one hundred euros), make love (afternoon sex was more of the throw-you-down/pull-your-hair type), nap, and then dinner at Maya's (Garrett knew almost every person at each table, and I recognized most of their faces from the pages of the gossip rags), and then a party on a different billionaire's boat. One night there was a "White Christmas" themed party and the entire top deck of the mega yacht had been covered in cotton balls to look like snow. And on another, we were invited to a yacht the size of a skyscraper turned on its side for a laser show (yes, you heard me correctly, a laser show).

At first I'd felt unworldly and unkempt, but Garrett had a way of treating me like I was the most beautiful woman in the room, even in the tall, thin, and tan celebrity-filled crowd here in St. Barts. He held my hand at every party we attended, giving me subtle squeezes all through the night, as if he was the lucky one in this duo. He seemed proud to be with me, and I felt safe with him, like he would always have my back. New York seemed a million miles away, and I wished we could stay right here in this very moment forever.

We toasted our last sunset with a glass of champagne.

"I never want a sunset without you, Emma," Garrett said.

My heart caught for a second, and he seemed poised to say something more. I raised my eyebrows.

Garrett chucked me under my chin. "We'd better get going, don't want to be late for dinner."

~~~~~

That evening's New Year's Eve party was the biggest of the week, and it would be capped with fireworks at midnight.

The giant yacht—so big it actually dwarfed Riley's—was docked at the harbor and hordes of glamorous people were boarding as we pulled up in our dinghy. I had seen more celebrities than I could count this week, and every single one of them seemed to be converging on this one yacht. And they were joined by every other master of the universe and socialite in St. Barts. I wondered what the percentage of the world's wealth was in that harbor.

Garrett pulled me into the fray and everyone greeted him warmly whether he knew them or not. We had a deal that if he didn't introduce me to whomever he was talking to, then it was understood that he had no idea what the person's name was and I had to introduce myself, which I did on cue each time. As smooth and garrulous as Garrett seemed to be, I knew this was as much a job for him as it was enjoyable. And my job was to stand by his side.

After a few hours of this, I'd had too much champagne and not enough food, and the crush got to me. My brain was swimming and that old feeling of unreality was washing over me again. When it was time for the fireworks, the entire crowd met on the right side of the boat for the best view. The weight of all that humanity actually tilted the boat in the water, and I looked down at my feet—one foot was higher than the other, and I wasn't standing on steps.

Garrett pulled me toward him. "You're not having any fun, are you?"

I shook my head, but not terribly convincingly. "I'm fine."

Garrett took my hand. "Let's get out of here." He held my sweaty palm as we walked down the steps and off the boat onto the dock. We heard the crowd start the countdown to the New Year, and he stopped and took me in his arms.

"I love you, Emma Guthrie," he said. Then he kissed me— gently, sweetly. And for just that moment, we were all alone.

## 7

I didn't think I had ever been so tired, not even when I'd worked sixteen hours straight on set. That was physical exhaustion. This was more than that. I had slept plenty in St. Barts, and it would be ludicrous to complain about constantly attentive service and endless visitors and parties. And yet . . . I would have complained if there were anyone sympathetic to listen.

After my initial shock, I'd eased into the rhythm of St. Barts over the next few days, and I'd grown genuinely fond of Riley. She even whisked me away for a quiet lunch once, just the two of us and a bottle of rosé. I'd been able to confide in her more than anyone except for Grace—and she had one thing that Grace didn't: She knew how to live on a yacht. In fact, Riley pretty much knew everything about everything, at least where beauty, fashion, sex, and gossip were concerned. She was like a little black book of information, telling me where to get my hair cut, the best personal shopper at Bergdorf, that it was time I started microdermabrasion to "maintain." I filed most of this information under "entertaining but not necessarily applicable." After this trip, it was back to H&M for me, and I'd be washing my own face, thank you very much. But if I ever did come into money, I'd know just who to call to help me learn how to spend it. Speaking of which, she knew exactly how much money everyone had—or didn't have. I totally cracked up when she sympathetically referred to one media titan as being down to his "last couple hundred million" from the one and a half billion *Forbes* had reported he had the year before. Riley also explained that she chose her friends carefully—she said she could practically smell the difference between someone who was genuine and someone who was just looking to climb the social ladder—and since I was dating Garrett I should learn to put my guard up as well. ("You'd better get a thick skin," she told me. "And get it fast.") According to Riley, New York was crawling with wannabe socialites who looked for any opportunity to attach themselves to people of power. She filled me in on who to avoid, giving me all of her tips on how to gracefully dodge the "glommers." It sounded like she thought of everything—even how to avoid having her picture printed with someone she found undesirable: She simply looked down as the photo was snapped, making it less likely to be published.

I was quiet on the flight back to Manhattan. Truthfully, part of me was glad to be going home to my apartment. No one would be bringing me fresh fruit for breakfast or waiting by the door with cold towels, but that also meant no one would walk in on me in my pajamas if they weren't invited or didn't already live there. Garrett was thumbing away on his phone, so, thankfully, conversation wasn't necessary. I looked at him and studied his face, his brows gently furrowed as he read, his mouth slightly open. He had told me he loved me, and I truly loved him. So how could I feel so exhausted, so worn-out, after that? I should be exhilarated, but instead I felt overwhelmed, like I needed a vacation—a real one this time. I stared out the window of the plane, preoccupied, and then felt Garrett reach for my hand. "Hey you. Penny for your thoughts. What are you thinking about?"

I smiled. "Nothing. Just tired. Ready to go home."

One of his eyebrows cocked in concern. "Ready to get rid of me?"

"No! God, no. It's just, I don't know how you do it. Being *on* all the time that way. I wish I were better at it."

Garrett reached out and pushed a loose strand of hair behind my ear. "I don't wish that. I like that you're different. And if you don't like parties, we don't have to go to them. Next Christmas we'll go to the Arctic Circle, how about that? No parties."

I smiled. "You're too good to me."

"I like those diamonds in your ears." He gently touched my earlobe.

"A really nice guy gave them to me," I said.

"Really. What's he like?"

"Well, he's a movie star. But that's not why I love him." I looked out the window.

"Why do you love him?" Garrett tugged a lock of my hair to get me to look back at him.

"Because he's kind. And interesting. And his face is lopsided. And he makes me feel safe."

"Safe is good?" Garrett looked interested.

"It can never be overrated."

"Emma, what if I wanted to make you feel safe all the time. And totally taken care of?"

My heart seized for a second in my chest and then it thumped loudly in my ears. "I'd say that sounds nice, and what do you mean?"

"I mean . . . move in with me, Emma. I don't want to say goodbye when we get to New York. I feel good when I'm with you. I feel at home. I can't remember the last time I felt at home anywhere."

Garrett was looking at me so seriously that I wasn't sure how many seconds passed before I could speak. "Garrett, I would love to, but . . . isn't this fast? It feels fast."

"Emma, I'm thirty-eight years old. I don't need a year to figure this out. I know what I want."

"Listen, I love you. More than I've loved anyone. And maybe that's part of the problem. What if you leave me? What then? I move out of your hotel and back to my apartment? That doesn't make me feel safe at all."

Garrett nodded his head gravely and then looked straight ahead. "I understand."

~~~~~

Garrett was sweetly attentive in the airport, but then two cars arrived, and I realized that one was for me and one was for him. He wasn't taking me home. I'd ruined everything. But what was my choice? Move in with him and swallow all my fears as if they didn't exist? I couldn't do that. And how could he expect me to?

I knew how. It was because he was used to having everything his way. I'd seen that in the last week. Waters parted for Garrett Walker. Nothing ruffled him, because nothing was allowed to.

And yet, he loved me. And he didn't have to. He could have taken some model to St. Barts with him, and it probably would have been a lot easier for him. But instead he took me. Shouldn't that count for something? All the way back to my apartment my thoughts bounced back and forth as if Garrett and I were on opposite sides of a tennis match. A running list of pros and cons.

It was late afternoon when the car pulled up to my building. The driver offered to carry my bags up, but I told him I was fine. The building was quiet, as if everyone was sleeping off the good cheer of the night before. I should have been doing the same, but my New Year's kiss with Garrett seemed like a lifetime ago and a world away.

When I unlocked the door, Lily was sprawled on the sofa in her pajamas watching *Clueless* on TV.

"Oh my God, you have no idea how good that looks to me right now," I said.

"Emma! Welcome home!" Lily launched herself off the sofa and gave me a hug. "God, I missed you. It's been boring as hell around here."

I pulled off my coat, kicked off my boots, and settled in next to her on the sofa. She clicked off the TV. "Boredom sounds so good to me right now."

"What's wrong, Emms? Didn't you have a good time?"

I rested my head on the back of the sofa with my eyes closed and sighed. "It's a little complicated."

"Holy . . . those are some serious rocks you have in your ears. A little Christmas present from Garrett?"

"Uh huh." I smiled. Lily didn't want to hear about complications.

"I saved all the paparazzi pics of you guys from the paper," she said, waiting for me to tell her more.

"Let me get unpacked, and then maybe we can order in?"

I dragged my bags into the bedroom and began to unpack everything. I'd forgotten how much I bought in St. Bart's. The caftans and evening dresses looked ridiculous next to my jeans and boots, but Lily squealed with delight as I unveiled every new purchase.

"Here, Lily, I got you this." I handed her a box, and she pulled out gold chandelier earrings with tiny multicolored gems that shimmered like rainbows in the light. I'd bought them for her with Garrett's credit card, but I knew he wouldn't mind.

Her eyes widened. "Oh my God, Emma, they're beautiful." She put them on right away and modeled them in the mirror. "They're not just beautiful, they're *fabulous*. We've got to go out and show them off."

I groaned. I was so looking forward to our sofa and Chinese delivery. "Oh honey, you go without me. I can't. I'm just beat." Lily picked up one of the tunics I'd bought at Calypso, and then pulled on some skinny jeans and boots. With the earrings, she looked fantastic.

"Pleeeeeease? Pretty, pretty please? I've been stuck here for days while you've been sailing the oceans blue. Take pity!" Lily held her hands up in prayer.

I laughed. "Oh my God, I can't believe you're making me do this. Fine. One drink." I held up my index finger. "Just one. And then you can stay if you want to, but I'm coming home and putting on pajamas, and not you or anyone else can stop me. Agreed?"

Lily jumped up and down like a little girl while I headed to the shower and tried to reassemble the Emma Guthrie I was before I went to St. Barts. I twisted my wet hair in a bun and pulled on my favorite jeans and boots. Then I looked in the mirror and caught sight of the diamond studs Garrett had given me, glinting in the light. They stood out as decidedly post–St. Barts, but they also distracted from the exhaustion on my wan face.

I grabbed my purse and coat, and the two of us took the stairs two at a time instead of waiting for the elevator. It was good to be with Lily. This was how it always used to be, when she'd drag me out to some bar and I'd have fun despite myself.

We spilled onto the street and then realized we had no idea where we were going, and it was too cold to wander. While we debated between Lily's idea of a good bar and mine, a dark car pulled up in front of our building. Then a familiar form emerged, and Lily gasped.

Garrett walked toward me. He nodded at Lily and smiled tightly.

"Garrett, this is my roommate, Lily, you've heard me talk about her."

Lily overcame her shock and turned smooth. "It's so great to meet you finally." She swung her long wavy hair and her new earrings glinted in the streetlight. "Emma has told me so much about you."

Not true, and Garrett knew it, but he let that pass with a debonair smile. "Lily, would you mind very much giving Emma and me a moment?"

Lily glanced at me uncertainly, and I'm sure I looked as confused as I felt. "Of course. I'll just step inside," she said. "It's kind of cold out here." Garrett's eyes followed her safely inside, where she stood watching us through the glass door. I never took my eyes off him. He was about to break up with me, I knew it. He couldn't wait until tomorrow, but he had too much class to do it over the phone. Or, God forbid, by text.

I looked at Lily and I saw her eyes widen in shock. I turned back to Garrett—and he was down on the sidewalk. He was kneeling. Oh my God, he was kneeling in front of me.

"Emma Guthrie, would you marry me?" Garrett's eyes were doing their sparkle dance, and he held a small black box in his hand. He opened it and pulled out a diamond ring with more carats than I could count.

I was going to faint. Garrett took my hand and grinned up at me, completely unfazed by my inability to speak. He slid the ring on my helpless hand. "I'm going to say it again, and I'm going to keep saying it until the answer is yes. Emma Guthrie, will you marry me?"

A dozen images flashed in my mind. They were a jumble of contradictions, and the two biggest were me and Garrett. And then I looked in his deep brown eyes and imagined him never looking at me that way again. And there was only one answer. But I said it three times just to be sure.

"Yes. Yes. Yes."

## 8

"You're getting *married*?" Mikey's normally excitable delivery had ratcheted up to a full-on shriek and I had to hold the phone away from my ear. Amazingly, he was genuinely shocked. I'd sworn Lily to secrecy the night before, but I couldn't imagine the level of self-discipline she'd exerted not to call Mikey and spill.

"Yes, she's getting *married*!" Lily yelled back from across the room, where the volume of Mikey's voice had carried. She'd had about eighteen hours to move past shock, and now the wheels in her brain were turning swiftly to bridesmaid dresses. She'd already reminded me twice that she didn't look good in strapless, and I shouldn't even think of any color that someone on earth might describe as yellow.

"I can't believe it, either," I said to Mikey. "And I'm the one getting married."

*Married.* Even the word felt foreign in my mouth, and the more times I said it the more strange it sounded. And the words *wife* and *husband* didn't feel any more natural. When I was looking at Garrett, and I'd said yes, I had managed to push all the logic of this decision out of my mind. Now my head was spinning with how quickly logic was rushing back in.

"When can we go *dress shopping?*" Mikey shrieked again.

"Just calm down," I said laughing. "Let's not get ahead of ourselves. And don't tell anybody I'm engaged." I turned to look over at Lily. "That goes for you, too. Garrett and I want to try to keep it a secret, at least for a week or so, so that we can talk to our families and get everyone used to the idea before the press gets ahold of it."

"Whatever, Emms," Mikey said. "I'll be over in twenty minutes with a stack of bridal magazines. We have a dress to discuss." I heard a click, and Mikey was gone.

After Garrett proposed, we went back to his hotel and spent a blissful night, just the two of us in our private, romantic cocoon. We stayed up late talking about the wedding, who we'd invite (my list consisted of family and a few friends; his consisted of every A-list name in Hollywood), and where we'd go on our honeymoon. We decided—really, Garrett decided, but I loved the idea—that Paris was the perfect place. I'd never been there before, and he looked wide-eyed with wonder when he talked about the first time he'd been to Paris. "You'll love it," he said. "I can't wait to show it to you." Then we pawed each other like hormonally charged teenagers, until I accidentally scratched his face with my rock of an engagement ring.

Garrett had whisked me away so quickly the night before that Lily hadn't even gotten a good look at the ring. When I came back the next morning, her mouth fell open at the sight of it. Neither of us had ever seen anything like it. I felt like I was wearing one of the British crown jewels on my finger, or a work of art that should have been in a museum somewhere. It was an old mine-cut diamond, round and larger than any real stone I'd ever seen, and it was set in platinum. The setting threaded around the base of the diamond, and each thread was also set with diamonds, as was the thin band of the ring itself. The stone was bold and bright—just like Garrett—but the setting was what made me love it. It was delicate and organic at the same time, and Garrett told me it was the only ring he'd seen that was good enough for me.

By the time I made my call to Mikey, Garrett was already jetting off to L.A. for meetings. He asked me to go with him, but I had too much to do, starting with calling my mother, my grandparents, and Grace, in that order, and I'd feel strange doing that from a private plane. Two days and nights in my little apartment with Lily and Mikey sounded blissful to me right now.

"Chinese?" I asked Lily.

"Duh."

The Chinese food delivery arrived before Mikey did, and I was halfway through my first egg roll when he burst through the door with a boat bag full of magazines.

"What is *that?*" he asked, pointing at the egg roll.

I wiped some hot mustard from my chin and looked at him quizzically.

"Emma," he said in a stern tone. "Put down the egg roll. You

have no business eating that way. And give me your phone—
I'm taking Suzie Wong off your speed dial."

"Oh please, Mikey," I said. "I'm not going to turn into one
of those women who don't eat before their wedding."

"Emms, you'd better get used to this now. We're not just
talking about your wedding here, we're talking about your
life. You *cannot* get fat."

"Michael, she's not fat!" Lily said in my defense.

"Of course she's not fat! I'm just saying she can't ever *get*
fat," he said.

"Well, that's true," Lily said.

"Why are we talking about me like I'm not here?" I said.
"And I'm gonna finish my damn egg roll, just so we're clear."

After a couple of hours of tearing out pages from bridal
magazines, I called it a night and went to bed. As I sank into
my familiar mattress—the first time I'd done so in weeks, I
realized—I wanted to fall into a dreamless sleep. But I heard
the murmur of Lily's and Mikey's voices in the living room,
and my thoughts turned back to the conversation I'd had with
my mother the night before I went to St. Barts.

I hadn't called Mom yet to tell her the news of my engagement, and the significance of that fact hadn't escaped me.
Shouldn't I have been on the phone with her the second
after Garrett proposed? Shouldn't he and I have called her
together, from the hotel that night? Why hadn't that even
occurred to me? I answered my own question: Because Mom
wasn't wrong—Garrett was from a different planet than my
family. Sure, at one time he had Christmas dinner in his mother's shabby living room just like I did. But those days were
long behind him, and I suspected the memory gave him no
pleasure.

I was certain of two things: I loved Garrett, and I wanted to marry him. But I wasn't at all certain I was ready for all the changes that would come with being Mrs. Garrett Walker. And I knew only one person who could possibly understand what I was going through.

I got up, turned on my computer, and logged into my email.

Hey Riley—Any chance you're free for lunch or coffee tomorrow? I have some news I want to share with you. And I need some advice.

xoEmma

A tall, thin blond girl stood behind the hostess booth at Michael's Restaurant. She looked me up and down and then her eyes settled on mine. Her stare was so disconcertingly long and intense that I wondered if she was able to scan my retinas to determine my relative status in the room.

"Good afternoon. May I help you?" she asked. Her demeanor was superficially pleasant, but underneath I caught a distinct whiff of superiority.

"Um, yes," I said. "I'm meeting someone. Riley Schwartz?"

A man in an impeccable suit rushed over. "You must be Miss Guthrie. We're so happy you and Mrs. Schwartz are joining us for lunch today. Her office just called and she's running a few minutes late. Amanda, take Miss Guthrie's coat. Champagne while you wait, Miss Guthrie?" He was so smooth that I was coatless and sitting down with a flute of bubbly in front of me before I'd said one more word.

I was speechless in any case, because he'd escorted me past

Barbara Walters, André Leon Talley (Mikey would die), and Michael Bloomberg. I didn't know what shocked me more—the sea of upper-echelon faces, or the fact that I actually recognized several of them from St. Barts. I felt a few eyes on me and wondered if they recognized me as well. I put my hands in my lap and turned my diamond to my palm. So much for a quiet lunch with Riley, but I guess in her world there was no such thing.

Luckily, I always carried a book for subway rides, so I had something to read while I waited for Riley and sipped champagne. A few minutes later, I heard a commotion—lots of loud "Hi-iiiiis" and "Daaaarlings"—and I looked up to see Riley in a classic gray tweed Chanel jacket and black leather pants, her perfectly coiffed, long red hair swinging back and forth as she trailed a series of air kisses across the dining room.

Finally she made it over to our table. "Hello, darling!" she said, her arms wide open for a hug.

After we exchanged greetings, and the same maître d' who had brought me to the table delivered another round of champagne, Riley tipped her chin down and said in a low voice, "Since you're drinking, I know you're not pregnant, and judging by that ring you have turned around backward on your finger, you must be engaged?"

Riley did not miss a trick. "Tell me the truth, Riley, do you have laser vision, or did you already know?"

She smiled, looking uncharacteristically prim and distinctly self-satisfied. "I had a feeling. I've known Garrett for years, and I've seen him with many different women and heard all of his antimarriage proclamations. With you, he was different." Then Riley held out her hand, palm up, and waggled her fingers. "Come on now. Let me see it."

I turned the ring around and held my hand down to the side of the table to hide it from anyone who might be looking.

"Oh, Emma," she said. "That is stunning—is it JAR?"

"How did you know?"

"Oh, there's no one like JAR. You can't mistake his jewelry for anyone else's. Anybody can have a diamond from Harry Winston, but JAR, now that is really special." I didn't think anything could impress Riley, but she seemed almost as giddy as Mikey.

After she'd loosened me up with several glasses of champagne, Riley gave me a pointed look and said, "Do you know what you're doing?"

My stomach rose uncomfortably close to my throat. Was Riley really doubting that I should marry Garrett? Did he have some kind of dark secret that I didn't know? "What . . . what do you mean?"

"The wedding, silly. Do you know what you're doing for a wedding planner?"

My heart thumped loudly in my chest and I realized that it must have stopped for a good ten seconds. "Oh, that. Well, that's what I wanted to ask you about. I don't really know where to start with the whole wedding thing. I didn't even have a boyfriend six months ago, and now I'm getting married. And planning a wedding in New York is a lot different than planning a wedding in Kentucky."

At that moment our waiter came to take our orders. I thought about what Mikey said and copied Riley's order exactly—a Cobb salad, no bacon, no egg yolks, no cheese, and the dressing on the side.

Riley didn't skip a beat and picked up right where the conversation left off. "Planning a New York wedding isn't the hard part. You're planning a celebrity wedding, and that is a horse of a different color altogether." She patted my hand. "I'm setting you up with the wedding planner I used. She knows what to do. She'll see to all the confidentiality agreements."

I looked at her, a blank expression on my face.

"You have no idea what I'm talking about, do you?" Riley said. "You'll need a confidentiality agreement from everyone—from the florist to the busboys. You don't want every detail of your wedding in *US Weekly* before it even takes place."

"Of course," I said, nodding knowingly, while inside I was wishing I had a pen to start taking notes.

"When do you want to get married? Next month? Next summer? The longer you wait, the more the press will dig. Do you want Oscar to design your dress? I can make a call. Do you see it in a church? In the city? In the country? Big or small?"

My answers couldn't keep up with her questions, but that didn't even slow her down. Finally, she took pity on me. "I'll have my assistant book an appointment with the wedding planner tomorrow," Riley announced. "You can meet with her at my apartment before Garrett gets back from L.A. Plan on two o'clock."

By the end of the lunch, I was more exhausted and more confused than before. The wedding didn't sound like fun—it sounded like work, and it was feeling like St. Barts all over again. But how could I possibly complain about this? Shouldn't it be my dream?

"Emma, I'm going to give you the best advice I can, and it's something that Garrett won't think to tell you, and it's something that would never occur to you to want. But believe me, you need it, and once you have it you'll wonder how you ever lived without it."

"Riley, if you're talking about a Brazilian wax, I'm covered."

Riley nearly spit out her champagne. "Oh honey, we are going to be good friends. No, it's not a Brazilian. What you need is an assistant."

~~~~~

It must have been the liquid courage of all that champagne at lunch that propelled me to call my mom when I got back to my apartment. I told her about the trip, leaving out the parts about all of the waitstaff and crazy extravagances, and peppered it with a few boldfaced names I knew she would enjoy hearing about. She asked how I liked being with Garrett for a whole week, and I knew that was the time to tell her.

It went as well as I could have expected, I guess, but I couldn't help wishing it didn't feel so awkward. I'd always pictured that when I got engaged, my mom would actually know the guy I was marrying, and that we'd call her together, and that it'd be one big lovefest. Instead it was just me, and there was a noticeable pause on the line before she told me how happy she was for me. I asked her to pass along the news to my grandparents and Maureen. She was so stunned by the turn of events that she didn't even ask me when the wedding would be.

~~~~~

"Emma, wake up." Lily poked me hard in the upper arm.

"What, what's going on?" I said groggily.

"There are photographers outside," she said. "It's in Page Six this morning that you were at lunch yesterday with Riley Schwartz showing her your engagement ring."

I shot up out of bed like I'd been hit with a Taser. *Shit.* Somebody must have overheard us talking. How could this have happened? Thank God I'd already told my mother.

But Mom wasn't the problem now. It was Garrett. He'd be furious. It wasn't even 5 a.m. and, in a panic, I called him in L.A., waking him. Near hysterics, I could barely get out the words.

"Well, it was bound to happen sooner or later," he said with ease. "Don't be upset, honey. It's not the end of the world. They'll get bored of us soon. In the meantime just enjoy the attention while you can."

"Enjoy the attention?" This was not the reaction I was expecting. I thought Garrett would be angry, but he sounded completely unconcerned. "So you're not mad?"

"Mad?" He laughed. "Of course not. Honey, I know it's got to be upsetting to wake up to photographers outside. And I know you're not used to this. We wanted to keep it quiet a little longer, but this is the way it goes for me. This is the life of a celebrity. Nothing's sacred."

"Okay. Sorry I woke you. I'll be fine."

"See you soon. Smile pretty for the paparazzi. I love you."

My next call was to Riley.

"Schwartz residence."

"Hi, this is Emma Guthrie calling for Riley."

"One moment please, Ms. Guthrie."

I waited a long minute, and then Riley sang into the phone. "Emma, I am soooooo sorry!" she said. "I just feel awful. I am so damn loud sometimes—you have to be so careful. Have you gotten a million phone calls?"

"No, but there are photographers outside my building," I said. "I'm kind of freaking out."

"Well, those people have willpower. They'll wait there until they get a shot of you. But once they do, they'll go away. It's probably better if you just go out and let them get their picture, but you have to look your best," she said with authority. "I'm going to send my hairstylist down to you and some clothes for you to choose from. The photo will run everywhere, you know, and you don't want to be haunted forever by a bad outfit."

Of course, in her wisdom Lily had already come to the same conclusion and called Mikey even before she'd awakened me. Within an hour he arrived on the heels of Riley's hairstylist and an assistant who was carrying two garment bags, stuffed to the brim. The hairstylist set about blow-drying my hair and setting it in rollers the size of soup cans while Mikey gasped his way through the clothes, announcing the designer of each piece ("Dior! Chloe! Armani! Ralph Lauren! A Birkin bag!").

"Okay," Mikey said after he got his wits about him. "You need to look casual, yet chic, a little more grown-up, but not too much. And not like you tried: Your look should be effortless. Put this on."

We were on outfit number three, a cream Ralph Lauren sweater, my own jeans, and a long gray Marc Jacobs coat with a paisley Etro scarf. Mikey stepped back and gave me his best thinking-man pose, studying me head to toe as he determined shoe choice.

"Where are those slouchy boots you wore when we went to meet what's-his-name at that art show in Brooklyn?" he asked. "Those would work. And where are those big sunglasses you bought in St. Barts? Oh, and of course, carry the Birkin."

"Yes, of course, Mikey, the Birkin," I said, rolling my eyes.

"Don't get saucy with me, Bernaise," he quipped in reply, doing his best Harvey Korman.

Once I had all the pieces put together and got Mikey's seal of approval, it was time to go face the paparazzi. It was only a few feet between my front door and the SUV that Riley had sent to take me to her apartment for my meeting with the wedding planner, but it felt like a city block. Riley told me that all I had to do was walk out, smile, and get in the car. I shouldn't look like I was posing, but I shouldn't look ashamed, either. Riley had said, "Head up, Emma. No looking at the ground."

Mikey gave me a big hug and spoke in a soft tone he reserved for rare tender moments. "Emms, you look beautiful. Now go out there and let the rest of the world see how lucky Garrett Walker is to have *you.*"

Deep breath, in and out. I got on the elevator and watched the doors close as Mikey and Lily waved goodbye. "We'll be watching through the window!" Lily called out just as the doors shut.

My stomach flitted with a thousand butterflies and my knees felt weak as I pushed open the front door. There were about ten photographers and a couple of camera crews waiting for me.

"Emma, Emma, right here!" they were each calling. "Emma, show us your ring! Emma, when's the wedding? Emma, how did you get Garrett Walker to propose?"

I smiled, my lips quivering, gave a timid wave, and got into the SUV. It was over. It took the entire ride, all the way to the Upper East Side, for my heart rate to slow back to normal. Even then I still didn't feel quite like myself. The driver opened my door and a butler was waiting with the door open to Riley's massive town house. I used to walk by mansions like this and peer in the windows at the décor, wondering what kind of people lived in them. (The kind of people who had butlers, that's who. And now I was becoming one of them.) The foyer had a double-height ceiling and marble floors, with a winding staircase that looked like it was made for a queen.

"Mrs. Schwartz will be with you shortly," the butler said to me. "Let me show you to the garden room."

The garden room was attached to a greenhouse and had floor-to-ceiling windows that looked out into a courtyard area. I didn't know places like this even existed in Manhattan. Then again, in my Manhattan, they didn't. I sat down on the sofa and sank into the soft down pillows covered in a giant leaf pattern. A woman in a maid's uniform wheeled in a cart with teapots, cups and saucers, a triple-tier stand filled with tiny sandwich triangles with the crusts removed, and a silver bucket with a bottle of chilled Dom Perignon.

"There she is," Riley exclaimed as she strode into the room. "The lady of the hour, our bride to be! Dara Durning, wedding planner extraordinaire, should be here soon. Meanwhile, let's have some champagne to celebrate. Maria, would you pour us some champagne? And do we have any of those little butter cookies? You know the ones I like from Sant Ambroeus?"

Maria poured us each a glass of champagne and in less than a minute another woman appeared with a plate of the butter cookies. I took one, but I noticed Riley didn't touch them. I nibbled one corner and left the rest on my plate.

Riley was talking a million miles a minute about ideas she had for the wedding (she'd clearly put more thought into this than I had), and I found myself looking longingly at the tea sandwiches. I could just hear Mikey scolding me, though. It was like I had a devil on one shoulder and an angel on the other, but I wasn't sure which one was Mikey.

The butler reappeared with Dara Durning. She looked cool and was dressed well but not intimidatingly so, more like an Upper East Side version of Stevie Nicks—nothing like the uptight, hyper-manicured women I'd met in St. Barts. On closer inspection, though, I detected an edge of intensity in her eyes, and I found myself sitting up straighter.

Dara asked all kinds of questions about my family, where I was from, and how I met Garrett. I felt like I was the one being interviewed for a job, not the reverse.

Thankfully, Riley cut off the twenty questions and got down to business. "Dara, I think she should use Preston Bailey for flowers, don't you? You should call and check his availability right away because it seems these days he's always off in the Middle East doing a twenty-million-dollar wedding for some sheikh's daughter. And Emma shouldn't have just any caterer," Riley continued. "It needs to be a renowned chef, like Daniel Boulud or Thomas Keller. Sylvia Weinstock for the cake, naturally."

Dara was feverishly scribbling notes on a legal pad.

"Then we need to discuss venue. Somewhere big, am I right, Emma?" Riley said, glancing at me but not giving me a minute to answer. "Garrett has so many colleagues he'll need to invite and I'm sure you have a lot of friends from back home, too.

"And what about the dress? Have you thought more about that?" This time she actually paused, and Dara looked up from her notepad awaiting my answer.

"Um, well, I think I'm going to let my friend Mikey, I mean Michael, choose," I said. "He's really into fashion." I could see the disappointment on both of their faces, so I quickly added, "But I would really appreciate your help in getting an appointment with a designer once we decide. And of course, your input would be great."

An hour later, I was thrilled when Riley said she had to cut our meeting short because she had to make it to a hair appointment at Warren-Tricomi. Dara told me she would email me a proposal that evening.

Garrett would be back from L.A. in a couple of hours, so I walked the few blocks from Riley's to the Carlyle hotel. The cold air burned my lungs and cooled down my hot cheeks. I hadn't even realized until I left how claustrophobic I'd been feeling. Now all I wanted to do was breathe.

I went up to Garrett's suite and took a hot bath, got into bed, and turned on the television. A couple of hours and a bad Lifetime movie later, I went downstairs and decided to check my email. Dara's proposal was waiting there for me.

Dear Emma,

It was such a pleasure meeting with you today. As promised, here is an estimated budget proposal for the wedding, not including dress or travel for guests. I am very much looking forward to working with you to plan your big day. My standard fee to coordinate an event of this magnitude is $80,000. A deposit of half is required as we begin, and the remaining balance will be due upon completion. After our discussion today, and in order to keep the wedding as private as possible, I think it is best to hold the event in a venue that has not been used for weddings before, as listed below. Please let me know if you have any questions.

Best,
Dara Durning

Guthrie/Walker Wedding

Venue Suggestion: 25 Broadway $50,000/day, 3-day rental

Carpeting and Draping of Walls in Venue: $100,000

Floral Design: approx $500,000

Dance Floor and Stage Construction: $25,000

Furniture Rental: $50,000

Food/Beverage: $400,000 ($1,000/person)

Security: $25,000

Cake: $10,000

Total: $1,340,000

*Holy shit.* More than a million dollars for a wedding. Stars burst around the edges of my vision, and my skin turned clammy. I put my head between my knees.

Was this really what I wanted? Or was this what I was *supposed* to want? Before I realized it, I was crying, and I didn't even know why. Garrett had told me he didn't care what we spent on the wedding, and Riley had even warned me that this is what celebrity weddings cost. So why did it all feel so . . . wrong? It wasn't even the money. I was a big girl. I knew that this was expected of Garrett, and he wasn't about to get married barefoot on a beach. But everything felt out of control, like the wedding was a runaway train and I was back at the station.

I heard the click of a key card and the door opened. "Hi, honey, I'm home," Garrett called.

I got up and ran to him, throwing my arms around his neck. He leaned back and looked at me carefully, then he kissed me, slowly backing me onto the sofa. We wrapped our arms and legs together until I wasn't sure which limbs were mine, and I tucked my head under his chin.

We lay that way awhile, and all the time my brain was churning, churning. I inched my way up and whispered in his ear. "Hey, baby, will you marry me?"

He pulled me even closer. "Of course."

"No, I mean will you marry me, like now?" I said. "Without all this hoopla?"

"You mean you want to elope?" His voice expressed surprise, and his hand stopped stroking my arm.

"Yes."

"Honey, I think that's really romantic, but don't you think your mom would be a little upset not to see her baby girl get married?"

"I guess you're right," I sighed and rolled up to a sitting position.

Garrett pulled me into his lap. "What's going on, Emma? Did the photographers scare you this morning?"

I shook my head. "No, it's not that. It's just that the whole time I was sitting in Riley's garden room today, everything felt out of control. And it's not that they weren't nice to me—they were. Riley's been amazing."

Garrett smiled at me. "But Riley was being pushy, right? And you didn't like feeling bossed around over your own wedding."

I groaned and flopped back on the sofa. "Exactly," I said. "I mean, every girl pictures her wedding day throughout her life, and granted, that picture changes over time. I know what I would want if it only mattered to you and me, but now I'm planning a wedding to suit the pages of *InStyle* and I don't want to embarrass you. Hell, where I come from, *fancy* means a ballroom at the Sheraton with an all-you-can-eat buffet and a DJ who brings his own Village People accessories." He laughed. I put both hands in front of my face and looked at him through the cracks between my fingers. "I'm being a child, right? I need to grow up and stop complaining."

Garrett reached over and pulled my hands away from my face. "What do *you* want? Forget about Riley and the wedding planner. What does Emma Guthrie, soon to be Emma Walker, want?"

That shut me up. I'd been feeling so put upon that I'd conveniently relinquished any responsibility for what I really did want. It was time for me to grow up, have an opinion, and take charge. I looked at Garrett. "I want a small wedding in a loft space downtown and I don't want a big princess dress. I want something sleek, and simple, and I don't want to have to starve to fit into it. And I want the food at the reception to be really good, and I want to eat a lot of it." There, I'd said it.

Garrett smiled. "Then that, my dear, is exactly what you shall have."

I threw my arms around him. "God, I love you."

"Me too, babe, me too." He stroked my hair from the top of my head to the tips and then he tugged on a strand. "Now that you mention really good food . . . I'm famished. I'm getting room service. You hungry?"

I thought back to that Cobb salad—no bacon, no yolks, no cheese, dressing on the side—and all those uneaten tea sandwiches with the crusts cut off. And I thought about the angel and the devil (both of whom looked like Mikey, for some reason) sitting on each of my shoulders. "Starving. Could you order me a turkey and bacon club, extra mayo, with fries?"

## 9

The interviewer for *People* magazine wasn't much older than me. Her name was Annalise and she wore dark jeans and a black blazer, black knee boots, black scarf, brown hair pulled into a ponytail. She looked like every other jaded New Yorker, and I have to admit it gave me a little thrill of satisfaction that she couldn't hide how impressed she was by our wedding.

It was late afternoon, the day after the wedding, and Annalise was grilling me for all the information they'd need for their cover story. Garrett's seen-it-all publicist, Alex, who was the only person I had ever witnessed tell Garrett what to do, had decided that we should give *People* exclusive wedding pictures in exchange for the cover, a six-page spread, and a tidy sum of money that Garrett donated to charity. At first I didn't like the idea of bartering our wedding pictures for flattering publicity, but Alex was blunt. She looked at me sharply and said, "Emma, if we don't write the story, then the tabloids and bloggers write it for us. And we may not like their version. It's either us or them—who do you want to be in control of the message?"

So here I sat in the living room of our suite in the Carlyle, the day after my storybook wedding, controlling the message. Garrett had begged off. Alex said, "This is the bride's thing. Nobody cares what the groom thinks, even if the groom is Garrett Walker." So he went off for drinks with his agent and a few other Hollywood power brokers, and I was stuck here with Broom-Hilda—I mean, Garrett's dear, sweet publicist.

At least I had some friends with me. When Lily heard that *People* was coming to interview me, she said she just had to be there. And I don't know how I would have managed every-thing over the last few days without Grace, so it felt like the most natural thing in the world to ask her to come, too. Truth-fully, once I was chatting away about the wedding, I started enjoying myself. I should have been exhausted from the wed-ding, but the adrenaline was still pumping, and I would have stopped strangers on the street to tell them about last night if I hadn't had a *People* reporter to tell—and Broom-Hilda here controlling the message.

Once Garrett and I had agreed to keep the wedding small, the problem of the invite list was the next thing to tackle. Alex said she was already dealing with an endless nightmare of phone calls and harangues for invites to the wedding. That got Dara's wheels turning, and she was the one who came up with the idea of making it a surprise wedding. I would have hugged her if I hadn't been so afraid of her.

We held it on Valentine's Day, just six weeks after Garrett proposed. Alex had made sure the word got out that we were taking our time and weren't setting a date until Garrett was done filming his next movie, due to start shooting in March.

Then we invited seventy-five friends and family to a party for our engagement—at least, that's what we told them. We flew everyone to New York, including my family, and this is when Grace showed her true colors. My mother was beside herself with nerves, and Maureen was a total pill as usual, and my grandparents didn't get around so easily anymore. Ideally, I would have been the one there to ease their minds and make all the arrangements, but I had to be in New York. I wasn't even planning the wedding, and yet somehow it had turned into a full-time job—as was meeting Garrett's entire social circle and attending endless lunches, dinners, and parties. Even dressing for a simple errand felt as complicated as preparing for a red-carpet event. Riley and Garrett had told me that the paparazzi would get bored, but instead they seemed to be getting hungrier for shots. Alex called it the Engagement Effect. She said once we got married we'd be less interesting.

So Grace took charge of the things that I couldn't. She was the only one—the only one—other than Alex and Dara who knew that we were throwing a surprise wedding. When push came to shove, I realized Grace was the one person other than Garrett whom I trusted most in the world. She got Maureen under control, she calmed my mother, and since I knew my mother wouldn't want some stranger from Dara's office barking instructions at her, she even coordinated their travel. Grace made sure that my grandfather didn't have to worry about walking too many steps in and out of buildings, and arranged activities and babysitters for my niece and nephews. Once they were all in New York, Grace played liaison with the personal shopper from Saks, who brought racks and racks of clothes for my family, Lily, and Grace to choose from, for what was supposed to be just a fancy engagement party. Grace gave my mother all the reassurance she needed about her hairstyle, the way the makeup artist had done her eyebrows—everything. And somehow she managed to keep Maureen away from me, without Maureen realizing it. For that alone Grace deserved a medal.

And when she wasn't corralling my family, Grace managed the final details of my wedding dress. Mikey had helped me choose it—I couldn't possibly turn my back on him in his hour of greatest need—but he thought the beautiful, drapey, winter white silk gown that we'd chosen for the wedding didn't need to be ready for months. So once again Grace came to the rescue. She played relay with Zac Posen's people, made up a story about how we needed it done for a pre-wedding photo shoot, wouldn't take no for an answer, and then came with me to my final fitting. I was so grateful that I insisted on buying her one of his dresses for the wedding. She tried to protest, but when she saw a flowered confection with a deep V and flouncy hemline, resistance was futile.

For the wedding, we rented the top three full-floor lofts of a building in Soho. It was one of those great old buildings that was once a factory and now was being converted to residential. The space was still raw, which I loved, and Dara had everything brought in to turn it into our own private wedding sanctuary.

As the guests arrived, the elevator doors opened up to a room decorated entirely in red. The guests were too busy air-kissing and catching up with each other to notice that the hostess wasn't there, Lily was happily mingling with the rich and famous and didn't think to miss me, and Grace told my family that I'd had a wardrobe malfunction and I'd be down soon. That was the only hairy moment—when Mikey caught wind that something was awry with my dress, he wanted to come find me immediately, and I still don't know how Grace managed to convince him not to. Then, midway through what seemed like nothing more than a lavish cocktail party, the guests were instructed to go upstairs. There they found a room draped in white fabric and dripping in white roses, lit only by candles.

An excited murmur began to spread among the guests, and my family was ushered to the front row, along with Lily, Mikey, and Grace. On the other side was Garrett's mother (whom I'd met for the first time just a few days before) with a few of her friends from home, alongside Garrett's agent and his wife, and a few of Garrett's closest friends (who happened to be A-list movie stars, directors, and producers).

During our vows, which Garrett and I wrote (he said I was his breath of fresh air, and I said he was my knight in shining armor—corny, but true), a crew transformed the cocktail space into a dining room, and a gorgeous dinner was prepared by Daniel Boulud. After all my talk about eating well at my wedding, of course, I barely touched a bite, and then we danced until midnight. Then Garrett whisked me back to the Carlyle, and we christened every room in the suite—including the foyer.

As I recounted *almost* every detail of the wedding night to Annalise, she was looking at me with rapt attention and I swear there was a tear in her eye.

"Oh my God, how did you keep it a secret that long?" she asked me.

"Well, I had lots of help. I couldn't have done any of this without my extraordinary wedding planner, and of course, Alex." I smiled sweetly over at Broom-Hilda.

"Were there any tricky moments when you thought the secret was out?" Annalise asked.

"Hmm, let me see." My brain was working now, because Alex was looking at me like a hawk. She'd prepared me for the interview, but this was one question we hadn't predicted.

Grace must have seen my distress, so she stepped in smoothly. "Emma, remember how your family was looking for you?"

I laughed. "Oh my God, yes." I smiled over at Grace. "Poor Grace. My mother was wondering where I was during the cocktail hour, but of course, I didn't want anyone to see me in my wedding dress, so Grace had to run interference. She told everyone that I'd had a wardrobe malfunction."

Annalise said, "That's fabulous! I love that story." Then she looked at Grace. "You're a friend of Emma's from back home?"

"Oh yeah, since diapers," Grace said laughing. "And even then I wore a larger size."

Even seen-it-all Alex laughed out loud at that line, and I could see that Annalise was thrilled at this heartwarming new angle for her story. Then I sensed a cold front immediately to my left, and I glanced over at Lily. She wasn't laughing. She wasn't even smiling. She looked at me, and then at Grace, and then at Annalise, and then she didn't look at me again for the rest of the interview, no matter how many times I tried to catch her eye.

Finally, Annalise said she had all she needed, and Alex escorted her out of the suite.

"So, Grace," Lily said. "When did you find out about the wedding?"

Grace looked confused for a second, and then awareness dawned: She wasn't supposed to know. No one was supposed to know. Lily had accepted that she'd been kept in the dark only because she thought everyone else had been, too.

"Lily," I said, "I needed Grace to help me with my family. Please don't be upset."

"I'm not upset." She smiled, but there was no emotion behind it. "Did you go to Emma's fitting with her, too? Is that where you got that Zac Posen you were wearing last night? I wondered about it, because I was sure that I hadn't seen it on that rack from Saks that I chose my dress from. Was that your reward for being so discreet?"

"Lily!" I was honestly upset now. I knew Lily could be self-centered, but this was taking things too far. It was my wedding, for God's sake. I was allowed to be a little selfish.

Alex charged back into the room. "Great job, Emma. And you too, Grace. Nice work." She looked at her watch. "All right, I've got to run. We'll talk later."

"Alex, we'll be on a plane to Paris for our honeymoon later. Talk to you when we get back?"

Alex rolled her eyes. "Do you really think you and Garrett are going to be able to turn off your phones for a week?" Then she headed for the door and waved at me over her shoulder. "Talk to you later, Emma."

Lily got up and followed Alex out. "Maybe I'll catch a ride. See you, ladies." And then she was gone. No kiss, no hug, no have-a-nice-honeymoon.

I was quiet for a few minutes after that, and I noticed that Grace hadn't said a word while Lily had her moment. "I blew it," I said. "I should have told Lily."

Grace looked at me thoughtfully. "Why didn't you? To be honest, I've been wondering."

"Well, Mom always told me, 'He who talks the most, loses the most,'" I said.

"But you told me," Grace pointed out.

"You don't count." I laughed. "We've shared a brain since childhood, remember? Obviously, I got the smaller half."

Grace threw a pillow at me. "You'll call Lily later and make up. It will be fine. Do you need help packing for Paris?"

"I'll have you know, I did that all by myself with my own two hands. When are you flying back to Kentucky?"

Grace sighed. "Tomorrow morning."

"You should stay longer—you didn't even get to sightsee, you've been so busy helping me. But I suppose Pete wants you back home. You never did tell me why he didn't come with you."

"Because I broke up with him," Grace said.

"Oh my God, Grace—why didn't you tell me?" Here she was fussing over every detail of my wedding after she'd broken up with the man she was supposed to marry.

"Because I didn't want to think about it. It was way more fun cruise-directing everyone else. Honest to God, Emma, I just couldn't take it anymore. Every night it was just me and him, a beer in his hand and his eyes glued to the TV. I had this vision of us fifty years from now in the same exact position, on the same ugly sofa, and I had a panic attack. I thought I was having a heart attack. Pete even drove me to the hospital, I was so scared. The good news for me was that I wasn't having a heart attack. The bad news for Pete was that I wasn't having a heart attack. But now it's time to go home and face the music. Move back in with Mom, I guess, until I find a place of my own. Let Jesus take the wheel." Then she smiled at me. "It'll be all right. Send me postcards from Paris!"

I looked at Grace, and it suddenly dawned on me: "Stay here."

"What are you talking about?"

"I mean, stay here in the suite while Garrett and I are away. Take a vacation. You deserve it. Then, when we come back, I want you to move up here for good. We'll find you an apartment."

"Emma, you're nuts. What kind of job am I going to find in Manhattan? I have no qualifications whatsoever."

"I wouldn't say that. It seems to me that you had Zac Posen's assistant at your beck and call, and I'm pretty sure that Broom-Hilda thinks you're heaven-sent. Look, Riley told me that I need an assistant, and I thought she was nuts at the time, but the last month has been insane. Alex was ready to skin me alive when I couldn't keep my calendar straight, and even Garrett has been telling me I need to hire someone. And you're the perfect person. I trust you more than anyone, and you're my best friend, and you want to get out of Kentucky. It's perfect. Just say yes."

Grace looked at me with such a serious face that for a second I thought she was going to cry. Then the corner of one side of her mouth turned up in a mischievous curl. "Hell, yes."

~~~~~~

Paris was . . . well, it was like tasting chocolate for the very first time, or seeing the ocean when you've only ever been landlocked. I felt as if a whole other universe were opening up to me, and all along it had been only a few hours away, I just didn't know it. For the first few days we didn't leave our suite in the George V, and I felt like Marie Antoinette—before everything went downhill for her. When we finally were ready to emerge into the sunlight, we spent the rest of the time visiting museums and flea markets, buying everything we fell in love with for the new home that Garrett promised we'd shop for once his next movie was behind him. We were followed by photographers here and there, but it was nothing like the cat-and-mouse game back home. Once they got their shot of us walking out of the hotel, they pretty much left us alone for the day.

At an elegant little stationers in the eighth arrondissement, I bought myself a new leather-bound journal, and that night, when we were relaxing in the suite before dinner (Garrett was taking me to Le Jules Verne in the Eiffel Tower), I started writing. I hadn't felt this free and inspired in months. I used to write every single day, for at least an hour (mostly because a professor had told me that you can't say you're a writer unless you write a page a day), all sorts of short stories, descriptions of people and places, and sometimes just bullet points outlining my days. But since I'd gotten the PA job, I'd barely picked up a pen and paper. In fact, since I'd met Garrett, I'd hardly thought twice about my career (or lack thereof). A brand-new journal was the perfect push to get me started again. An hour passed and I was still scribbling away, and finally Garrett said, "Hey, Hemingway, what are you working on?"

"A story," I said.

"What *kind* of story, dear?" He tickled my waist.

"It's a love story about a girl from Kentucky and the handsome movie star she falls in love with. Only in my story the girl's from Delaware, and the movie star is really, really ugly." I laughed as Garrett launched himself at me. "And he has bad breath!" Playfully he pinned my arms above my head and pretended to blow his bad breath at me, until . . . one thing led to another . . .

Approximately a half hour later, we were lying naked on our backs in bed, and Garrett was playing with the ends of my hair. "That story you're writing sounds like a movie."

I turned on my side and looked at him. "I was thinking the same thing. You know, that's what I've always wanted to do. I mean, I was a film major before I lost my scholarship."

"You could go back to school if you wanted to, honey. No scholarship needed this time," Garrett said.

I laughed. "Ah, but then I'd still have to fulfill my science requirement."

"Lazy." Garrett smiled.

I kissed him. "No, just spoiled."

Our honeymoon officially ended when a cell phone rang across the room. Garrett groaned. "Ugh. Whose is it, mine or yours?"

"Well, it's not mine. Who'd be calling me? It's got to be yours." Garrett had gotten out of bed to retrieve his cell, and I called after him, "It's probably your agent. He's lost without you. Positively bereft."

Garrett came back with a pointed smile. "Here you go, smarty." He handed me my cell phone.

"What? It's not home is it? Is everything all right?" I asked, suddenly worried.

"It's not home. It's Alex—for you."

When I said hello, Alex didn't reply with a "hi" or a "how are you," she just dived right into business. "I got us *Vogue*. You're going to be their 'It Girl' in the June issue. This is *huge*." Click.

I handed the phone back to Garrett. He smiled at me. "Come on, It Girl. Let's get you dressed. What would *Vogue* say if you went to dinner at Le Jules Verne in a sheet?"

———

It took barely an hour to find the apartment of Grace's dreams. She'd spent the week of my honeymoon walking around every neighborhood in the city, and she decided that the West Village was the place for her. With a general set of requirements, the real estate agent had shown us three apartments when Grace announced, "This is it."

She was right. It was adorable—a one-bedroom apartment with period molding and a claw-foot tub, and even a working fireplace. It wasn't big, but Grace didn't want big. I told the agent we'd take it, and she gleefully called the management company.

Grace lay down on the bare wood floor and smiled hugely. I smiled back at her. "I am so happy to see you happy."

I must have sounded a little wistful, because Grace's forehead wrinkled. "What's wrong, Emma? That sounded kind of sad."

I shook my head and sat down next to her. "Oh God, no, it's not that. It's just that for the last six weeks or so I've been so focused on the wedding and everything else that I conveniently managed to forget that I have no future plans. I mean, other than being Mrs. Walker."

Grace sat up. "Well it's not so bad being Mrs. Walker, right? I mean, I don't really need to list all the pros for you, do I?"

"No. There's not enough time in the day for that. I guess I'm just feeling aimless. I mean, I wake up in a hotel, my meals are brought to me, the most challenging decision I make on a daily basis is what to wear."

Grace nodded her head sympathetically. "And let's face it, Emma. Mikey tells you what to wear."

I hit her with my purse, and Grace laughed. "I have to make a call," she said. Then she dialed someone and gave them our current address.

"Who was that, the driver? I was thinking we could stroll around for a while. Maybe do some shopping and go out for a drink."

Grace smiled. "I can't. Got plans."

"What plans? I knew it—you met someone while I was in Paris?" She shook her head. "That hot photographer's assistant from the wedding? He was totally flirting with you. C'mon, spill!" She wasn't budging.

I teased Grace all the way downstairs. "Gracey has a da-ate, Gracey has a da-ate."

But when we spilled out on the street, it wasn't Grace's date, it was Garrett. "Come on, babe, I have something I want you to see."

Grace said goodbye with a Cheshire Cat smile on her face as we climbed into the car, and the driver headed even farther downtown. I decided not to ask Garrett any questions, because he was clearly enjoying his mystery mission.

"Babe, Alex called. I don't know why she didn't just call you directly. *Vogue* wants to know what you do, and she wasn't sure what to tell them." Garrett said this matter-of-factly, while scrolling through emails.

"What I do? I don't know. I guess I don't do anything right now."

"Mmmm. I don't think Alex is going to like that answer. Let's think about it this way: What do you *want* to do?"

"Well, I want to be a screenwriter. But I've barely started on the screenplay. I can't say I'm a screenwriter."

"Oh, sweetheart, if half the people in Hollywood approached their résumés that way they'd all have to admit they were waiters and not actors. If you're writing a screenplay, then you're a screenwriter. It's as simple as that."

I smiled at him. "I like that. I'm a screenwriter." I nodded my head. "I like that a lot."

"Just remember to thank me in your Oscar speech," Garrett said with a playful squeeze. "Don't forget the little people when you make it big."

The driver let us off in front of a huge building in Soho, obviously a former warehouse. Inside there was a large, cleanly designed lobby and a warmly debonair doorman who asked no questions.

I looked at Garrett quizzically, but I said nothing. As we entered the elevator, Garrett pulled out a set of keys that he used to light up the button for one of the top floors. "So," Garrett said while we climbed. "You like Soho, right?"

I nodded.

"And you like unfinished spaces in Soho, right?"

I nodded again.

"Big windows, high ceilings, lots of light. Am I getting all this right?"

"Uh huh," I said.

The elevator stopped and the doors opened. Garrett put his hand lightly at the base of my back. "Welcome home, Mrs. Walker."

In front of me was the space of my dreams—if I had dreams that big. It was totally unfinished, and it went on and on, and the light and views were spectacular.

Garrett said, "Obviously, it needs work. But I think it has potential." He looked at me with a merry glint in his eyes. "How about you?"

I laughed. "Uh, yeah, duh—I'd say it definitely has *potential*. You are insane, you know that? When did you have time to find this?"

"Grace helped. She's a doll, that one. Anyway, we'll need to hire an architect, but you should start thinking about what you want."

"Oh, I know what I want." I laughed. "You should see the stack of magazine clippings I've collected."

"Yeah, I've seen them. How do you think I knew what to buy?"

"So this is really ours? We *own* this?"

Garrett came up behind me and put his arms around my waist. "We do. Are you happy?"

I closed my eyes and felt the sunshine streaming through the windows, warm on my cheeks. "So happy."

# PART TWO

2010

## 10

There was barely a flush of pink in the dawn sky as I raced to the gym for my morning workout. You might think that I'd want to save my energy for the huge night ahead—the annual Met Costume Institute Gala, the event of the season. But no, I needed to get my butt kicked by a trainer at the Tracy Anderson gym. It was agony—a perfect combination of masochism (me) and sadism (my trainer). And I wasn't alone. Even at this early hour the gym was already populated by a sampling of tonight's gala attendees, all just as focused on the need to get into their dresses and not shame themselves under Anna Wintour's steely examination. Since most of us had also been starving ourselves for the last week, it's a wonder there weren't casualties.

After the training session, I was picked up in a black SUV by one of our full-time drivers and I pulled out my iPhone.

Thirty-two new emails in the last two hours. As always, I looked at Grace's emails first. She'd prioritize everything else for me, and also make sure I stayed on schedule.

Yo, Emms. You have an 8 a.m. call with Harvey Weinstein. Then I'll be at your place at 8:45 a.m. to pick you up for a 9:15 a.m. arrival at the Botanic Garden. Note that the writer will be at the shoot and interview will follow.—Grace

Then I read Garrett's email. Yes, I read my assistant's email before my husband's.

Hey babe,
   Wheels up. Be in NYC by 2. Late lunch? Can't wait to see you. Hope you're ready for me.
                                                            xxG

Oh, I was ready. He'd been on location in London for two months, and with the exception of a few rushed weekends, we'd been separated that entire time. I used to love going on location with Garrett—not just to see him in his element, but also to watch the director work. It was like an on-site film school, and I learned more in one day than I had in an entire semester of college.

But those days were over. There had been enough demands on my time when I was just Mrs. Walker—now I was Emma Walker, screenwriter. My first screenplay had turned into the hit romantic comedy of last summer. Writing it had come so easily to me—country bumpkin falls in love with movie star—and it took me by surprise when it became a hit. It even got some admiring reviews, which was a real achievement for a fluffy summer romance.

That was all great, but now expectations were enormous for my next screenplay, and Harvey Weinstein had bought it sight unseen. The thought of talking to him at 8 a.m. made my heart clench. He was expecting the screenplay any day now, and I hadn't written a word. Every time I turned on my computer and looked at the blank Word document, that old feeling of panic washed over me and I just wanted to go to sleep.

Somehow, I needed to buy myself more time.

Next email . . .

Emm:

Sorry I didn't stop by last night. Had a major monumental French consulate event at Jazz at Lincoln Center. Lasted forever. Thought the fitting yesterday was fabulous. The skirt so beautifully draped. So much like Madame Gres. I will go pick up the jewels at Fred Leighton. You must have the highest possible Manolos. The height of elegance—and your first instinct is always the correct one. You will be the essence of originality!

Good luck at the Vogue shoot. Wish I could be there!

You better have cut out the carbs.

Love,
Michael

Michael had gone from personal shopper at Barneys to fashion editor at *Vogue,* and his use of superlatives had only increased with each new promotion. The roster of women he styled these days was tiny and highly exclusive, but bless him, he always had time for me, and his enthusiasm for the task had never waned. Last year the Met ball theme was "superheroes" and he tried (unsuccessfully) to get me to wear a sequined leotard. This year he'd chosen a gorgeous Marchesa gown. The theme was "the goddess," and my dress was strong, yet feminine (his words, not mine), white with embroidered detailing that formed a golden bustier. His vision was a "modern-day Helen of Troy."

The car pulled up at our loft building and I jumped out quickly, already knowing that every second of my day—and more—was prescheduled for me.

When we left the gym, the driver had called ahead to our house manager just as he always did, and as the doors opened to the third floor of our apartment, my coffee—with soy milk, extra hot—was waiting for me on the table in the entryway. I grabbed the *New York Post* from the stack of papers, cruised down the hall to my office, and flipped on the light. The room looked more like the dressing room of a Parisian courtier than an office—the chandelier's soft glow reflecting off the antiqued silver-leaf walls, the sage green brushed-velvet cushioned chair—and I loved every inch of it. The centerpiece of the room was a dramatic black-and-white print of a Robert Mapplethorpe calla lily that Garrett had given me for my thirtieth birthday just a few months before.

I kicked off my shoes and peeled off my socks, running my toes through the plush rug, my back to a wall of windows looking out at the New York skyline. Then I quickly scanned Page Six to make sure there wasn't anything damaging about Garrett or any of our friends, my daily ritual. Nothing today, so there would be no frantic calls from Alex, and nothing to spin. Nor would I have to talk any of my friends off a publicity-driven ledge. Thank God.

I pressed the power button on my computer and scanned a piece on tonight's event. Apparently a stylist whom Anna didn't like had been banned.

The intercom buzzed, bringing me back to my own reality.

"Mrs. Walker, Harvey Weinstein is on line one."

I picked up the phone, the receiver feeling as heavy as the dumbbells I'd just been lifting, knowing the weight on the other end.

"Good morning, Harvey!" I sounded positive and perfectly at ease—I hoped.

"How's my script coming?" he bellowed.

"Really well," I said, exuding false confidence. I twisted one of my diamond stud earrings, the way I always did when I was anxious. "I just want it to be perfect before you see it."

"You know, Emma," he said, his volume lowering several notches, "I don't usually option unwritten scripts. Especially when I don't even know the plot."

"Harvey, honey," I replied, laying on the southern accent, so helpful at times like these, "you are going to love it. Promise."

"I need to read it. Soon."

"You will," I said brightly. "We'll see you tonight. I'm wearing one of Georgina's gowns."

My heart was thumping as I hung up and set the phone back in its cradle. I looked back at my computer screen and clicked on the folder marked "Untitled #2" and stared at the blank page. I started twisting the other earring.

Nothing. I had nothing. But there was no time to fret over it today. Between the photo shoot, Garrett coming home, and the ball, I would just have to start working on it tomorrow.

Unfortunately, excuses were coming to me more easily than words, and I looked at the clock and realized Grace would be there to pick me up for the *Vogue* shoot in twenty minutes. I rushed down the stairs to the master bedroom suite to take a quick shower.

By the time I'd thrown on a long-sleeved T-shirt, cashmere sweatpants, and twisted my hair in a haphazard bun (Michael would be horrified that I left the house like this), Grace was already at the elevator, holding the door so we wouldn't have to wait. She handed me a green juice and a printout of the day's itinerary.

"Do I really have to do this today?" I asked her.

"Yes, you really have to do this," she replied mockingly. "Do you know how many women would kill to be featured in a spread in *Vogue*'s Age issue? This is a real honor, Emma. Get it together."

It had been seven years since I was *Vogue*'s June It Girl, and that was nothing compared to the scene that met us when we arrived at the location of the photo shoot. We pulled up to the Brooklyn Botanic Garden and found four trailers lined up. One for the photographer and photo editors, one for catering, one for hair and makeup, and one for wardrobe.

"Patrick, this is like a movie production," I said to the legendary photographer as we air-kissed each cheek.

"My darling, so nice to see you," he replied in his French accent, as thick as Camembert.

A flustered, chicly dressed young assistant hurried us into the hair and makeup trailer. After exchanging over-the-top hellos with the glam squad, I plopped into a chair, ready to zone out for the next two hours as I was coiffed, curled, bronzed, concealed, and highlighted.

I started to daydream, relaxing into a gentle trance with the whir of the blow-dryer and the soft bristles of the brush against my scalp. I missed Garrett terribly, but I often felt a little anxious before he came home from a long shoot. There was always an adjustment period, a time of settling back into being a couple again. I had gotten very comfortable with going about my business—early to bed, early to rise—and he was used to working odd hours, socializing at even odder hours, and having someone to attend to his every beck and call. When he came back from an extended absence, we both had to learn to compromise again. We needed to reconnect, mentally and physically.

The buzz of my iPhone snapped me back to reality.

Emm:

At Fred. I've rethought the jewels. Please, please, I think the pearls with the diamonds is just too old. The pearls are going to look really dowager, pigeon crested. Although you do have the neck, but not with this look. You should only go with the diamonds that are a single strand like teardrops and a simple earring.

Are they treating you like the princess you are??

Love,
Michael

Immediately followed by:

Emm:

And did you get the Manolos? The messenger should have been there by this morning. You need to have a killer shoe for the red carpet. Meaning in looks, not pain.

-M

And yet another:

> You are going to look incredible. Incredible.
> -M

To which I replied:

> Michael:
> It's just a party.
>                                         xoE

Of course, even I knew it wasn't "just a party," but I couldn't resist the opportunity to get him all riled up. Still, it was taking a risk. It was entirely possible that upon receiving my blasé text, Michael would levitate himself to Brooklyn using the sheer force of his fashion anxiety—and slap some sense into me faster than he could hit SEND on yet another text. I tapped out another text.

> Just kidding . . . I'll wear whatever you tell me to wear. Xxoo

The photo shoot and interview concluded precisely on time (Anna ran a tight ship, I had to admire the level of organization), and the driver was waiting with the engine running to take me back to the apartment. Grace was inside with yet another itinerary—updated since this morning.

My phone rang and it was Garrett, nearly home from Teterboro.

"Hi, honey, how was the flight?"

"Oh, you know, the usual. Glad it's over," Garrett said.

Another call came in—it was Alex, über-publicist. "Shit, Garrett, would you hold on a minute?"

Grace looked at me with two raised eyebrows.

I switched to answer Alex's call. "Hey, Alex, what's up?"

"Harvey's office called and they want to know what you told *Vogue* about your screenplay," Alex said.

"The usual, that I was working on something exciting, but it was too early to talk about it." Then click, and she was gone.

And so was Garrett, it turned out. Well, that was okay. I'd see him soon enough.

Grace said, "You put Garrett on hold?"

"Yeah, why? Come on, Grace, he's my husband. He knows I'm working today. And God knows he's put me on hold plenty of times."

"Makes sense, it's just I know how he hates to be put on hold. That's all." Grace busied herself with her own phone and we didn't talk for the rest of the trip. The driver dropped me off at my door and Grace proceeded on with the car to pick up my Marchesa gown.

I flew through the open door and up to our penthouse, butterflies building in my stomach like it was my first date with Garrett.

When the doors opened into the apartment, I saw Garrett's iPhone on the foyer table and caught a trace of his familiar scent, like soap and tobacco.

"Good afternoon, Mrs. Walker." One of the housekeepers greeted me. "May I get you a cup of tea?"

"No, that's okay," I responded. "Is Garrett upstairs?"

"Yes, Mrs. Walker. He's sleeping and asked not to be disturbed."

I went up to my closet, took off my clothes, and changed into a pair of black lace boy shorts and tiptoed into the bedroom, careful not to wake him. I peeled back the sheet and got into bed, pressing my bare breasts against his naked back while gently kissing his ear.

Garrett rolled over and smiled. "Well, hello to you," he said slyly, before turning me on my back and holding my hands above my head. "We don't have much time, so let's make the most of it."

He kissed slowly down my neck, breasts, and stomach. He pulled my panties to the side and entered me. It was quick, and intense, and before I'd even caught my breath I popped out of bed and headed for the shower. I had to wash off today's hair and makeup to prepare for tonight's hair and makeup. Garrett joined me and I put my arms around him as the hot water poured down on us. I squeezed shower gel onto a sponge and turned Garrett around to wash his back. Swirling the suds on his muscles, I noticed a few scratches on his neck.

"Geez, baby," I said. "What happened back there?"

"War wounds. That shoot kicked my ass." He shut off the shower. "Come on, I want to give you your present." He pulled me out after him and we wrapped ourselves in towels. Then he presented me with a large pearly gray box with a gold satin ribbon.

I smiled. "What is this?"

"Just open it. And don't shake it first. That would not be good. I want you to know I picked this out myself. No assistants involved."

I pulled one end of the ribbon and lifted the top to reveal a breathtakingly lovely antique porcelain tea set. Ever since we'd gone to Paris for our honeymoon, I'd been collecting them, but this was the first time that Garrett had ever chosen one for me himself. "Garrett, it's gorgeous!" And it was, but it wasn't the present that made me so happy, it was the time he'd obviously taken to find it for me—and the thoughtfulness.

I carefully put the box aside and then leapt on Garrett, trying to wrestle him back down on the bed. Then he grunted— not jokingly. It sounded like real pain.

I pulled off of him quickly. "Honey, are you okay? Did I hurt you?"

"No, no. I bruised a rib last week and it's still not quite right." He lay back on the bed. "God, Emms, I'm getting old."

"You're not old! Don't even say that." I swatted his arm playfully. Garrett had turned forty-six the week before the shoot, and I knew it was bothering him that he was one year closer to fifty than forty.

"Well, tell that to Michael Bay. He passed me up for his next picture. I'm telling you, that part was written for me. But he found a younger, cheaper guy instead. The kind of guy who should be playing my sidekick." Garrett sighed and rubbed his eyes with the heels of his palms. "And that one has franchise written all over it."

"Oh, Garrett, I'm so sorry. But maybe it's for the best. You said yourself you were getting a little tired of action movies, right? All the training, and the crazy diet you have to go on before every shoot. And this last one sounds like it was miserable." I was stroking his chest lightly while I spoke to him, and I felt the muscles tense.

"Emma, if I'm not an action hero, then what am I?"

"Garrett, you're the hottest actor in Hollywood. No one can open a movie like you. And no one is more beloved than you."

"Beloved, huh? That's what they say about people right around the time they start giving them lifetime achievement awards."

"Stop it, Garrett, you know that's not what I meant."

"I know, babe, I know. And I love you for it. Now you'd better get your butt ready for the ball, Cinderella."

Michael's hair and makeup team arrived in minutes and it was a race to the finish line to get out the door to the waiting limo. The amount of labor—and people—that it took to get one woman (who was neither an actress nor a model) ready for a party was absurd. But I kept my smile bright, and I reminded myself that this was part of my job. Finally, as Garrett and I dashed into the elevator, Grace ran after us with our phones, which we'd both left behind. Garrett stuffed his phone in his jacket pocket, mine went in my purse, and then we were off.

~~~~~

If Grace hadn't handed me the wrong phone, I would have spent that evening by my husband's side, thrilled to have him back in town, and counting the minutes until I could lure him back home. Instead the night went by in a nauseated, light-headed haze. There were a few times that I was afraid I'd have to leave the table to go vomit in the bathroom. I wouldn't be the first person at the ball to purge after dinner, but that wasn't usually my style.

I felt so stupid, so embarrassed. Garrett sat next to me all evening, never leaving my side, always touching my hand and stroking my back. I'm sure he thought my reserve was due to my usual anxiety at large public events. That saved me from having to answer any of his questioning looks.

Garrett had pulled Lily toward him in the auditorium with the same practiced hand that he'd used to draw me to him. He'd flashed her the same mischievous, crooked smile. Now I replayed their kiss in my mind over, and over, and over again.

Pondering Garrett's betrayal was too much. I couldn't bear it. So instead I turned my thoughts to Lily. At one time I could never have suspected her of being capable of such a thing, but now I realized just how naïve I'd been. Over the years, we had grown apart the way many women do once they no longer have endless time to hang out on each other's sofas and dissect every detail of their romantic lives. She'd continued to work as an actress, but never quite made it to the level of star. In her bigger films, she was always the cute best friend. As we closed in on thirty, Lily had often complained that the pool of eligible men was scaling up in age, too. Of course, there were plenty of single men her age who would have given both legs to be with Lily, but Lily had champagne taste. A few years ago she told me that she had an older, married boyfriend— an executive producer on her latest film. I'm not sure how she expected me to react, but I guess I didn't hide my disapproval well enough, and she stopped confiding in me about men after that.

No, the question that haunted me now wasn't about my former best friend and how she could have done this to me. Her part in this was all too clear and predictable. What killed me was Garrett's part in all of this: How could he have done this to me?

I gave the performance of a lifetime through dinner. Honestly, I deserved an Academy Award for simply managing not to use my fork to gouge out Garrett's eyes. I remained calm, and Garrett acted as charming as ever, as if absolutely nothing had happened.

At the end of the ball, Garrett was keyed up and full of adrenaline. The cameras and attention exhausted me, but it all energized him, and he was ready to go out with friends to the after-party. I begged off, saying I had a headache, and he didn't seem terribly disappointed. I had been enough of a drag all evening that he must have realized he'd have a better time without me.

That night I lay in bed replaying the scene in the auditorium in my head. During those long, sleepless hours, I began to dissect their body language, gesture by gesture—clinically, punishingly. Clearly this wasn't the first time they'd been together. And if it wasn't the first time, when was the last time?

When I heard Garrett come in around 4 a.m., I pretended to be sleeping. I listened to the sound of the faucet running as he brushed his teeth, then his clothes as they hit the floor. He pulled up the covers and slid into bed next to me, rubbing his feet against mine and kissing my shoulder.

I lay there quietly, waiting to hear his breath slow. When I was sure he was deeply asleep, I slipped out of bed. I needed to find out how long this had been going on before I could fully accept the truth and confront either one of them. I thought about my mother putting me and my sister in the car and driving to the bank to get the evidence that my dad was cheating. She was humiliated, but at least she knew the truth. I needed to know the whole truth, too. I was my mother's daughter, and she always said, It's one thing to trust—it's another thing to be a fool.

Slowly I opened the door to our bedroom, careful not to wake Garrett. I went down the hallway to his office and found his laptop sitting open on his desk. I turned it on and clicked the mail icon. Garrett was not the most tech-savvy person, but I would have thought that even he would have a password to protect his email. But no, it was all sitting right there.

I clicked the FROM tab and scrolled down to see a whole string of emails from Lily—with replies from Garrett.

Hey Garrett,

I ran into an old friend of yours at a party the other night—Mark Lynch. Anyway, that made me think of you. How's the shoot going?

Xo,

Lily

Well hello Lily,

Pleasant surprise to hear from you. Shoot's going well, but I am currently flat on my back with an ice pack on my ankle. So much for doing my own stunts.

Best,

Garrett

Dear Garrett,

Poor you! Is anyone taking care of you? I'm so sorry!

Love,

Lily

Lily, you are very sweet. No one is taking care of me. I am all alone in my luxurious hotel suite, eating egg whites and drinking a protein shake (bleh, don't ask), with nothing but a remote control for company.

Xo,

Garrett

Poor, sad Garrett!

Is Emma on her way? I'm sure she must be very worried about you.

Love,
Lily

Lily,

I'm surprised Emma didn't tell you. I begged her to come to London with me, but she said she couldn't. She owes The Great Harvey a screenplay.

Best,
Garrett

Oh my God, Garrett, that's awful. I'm really shocked to hear that Emma isn't there for you. Sometimes I think she doesn't know how lucky she is. I would be there in a heartbeat, if I were her.

Love,
Lily

Sweetheart, it kills me to say it, but Emma has changed. She's not the girl I married. That girl would have dropped everything to come to London. The new Emma . . . not so much . . . you know? Guess it's partially my own fault . . . she wouldn't have her career if it weren't for me, but now her career is more important than me. It hurts. But you're sweet to care.

Love,
Garrett

Hey Garrett,

I know this is sudden, but my agent got me an audition for the new Guy Ritchie movie, and they want me to fly to London. How about dinner?

> Love,
> Lily

Well, Lily, that is a very nice offer. This shoot is keeping me very busy (when I'm not broken and bruised), but why don't you call me when you get here?

> Xo,
> Garrett

Five days had passed until the final email exchange, dated yesterday.

Garrett,

I'm lying in bed . . . can't stop thinking about you . . . your kiss, your touch . . . you drove me crazy.

I wish we never had to go back to New York.

I miss you.

> Love,
> Lily

Lying in bed are you? Me too.

Tell me more about what you're thinking . . .

> xxG

The emails went on and on . . . in graphic detail.

## 11

I leaned over and threw up in the wastebasket next to Garrett's desk. I couldn't even cry.

I went into his bathroom and flushed the vomit in the toilet. I splashed my face with cold water and sat down, stunned, on the cold marble floor. It was 6 a.m. and the sun was starting to rise. I picked up the bathroom phone and dialed.

"Schwartz residence," a deep man's voice answered.

"Hello, this is Emma Walker calling for Riley," I said, the quiver in my voice making the words barely intelligible.

"I'm sorry, Mrs. Walker, but Mrs. Schwartz is sleeping."

"Can you please wake her?" I replied. "It's urgent."

I nervously twisted my earring, and a few minutes later Riley came to the phone. "Emma, what's wrong?"

"It's Garrett," I said, struggling to get each word out, as the rock of sadness in my throat began to choke me. "He cheated on me with Lily."

No one was better in a time of crisis than Riley. "Emma, I'm so sorry. Listen . . . I know this is hard to hear and I'll comfort you later when we're together, but right now you need to be strategic. You need a lawyer. Right away. Does Garrett know you know?"

"No," I said in a small voice.

"Good, because you need to get a lawyer before you confront Garrett about *anything*. Do you understand me? Don't say a word to Garrett. Not yet."

"You mean I have to pretend I don't know? Riley, I can't do that. I can't even stand up I'm so devastated. I couldn't possibly look at him without crying or hitting him right now, let alone pretend everything's fine."

"Listen, Emma, Garrett has a team around him—lawyers on retainer, business managers, accountants, publicists. They will all look after him, because that's their job. He's the one who pays the bills. You need someone of your own right now."

"You really think I need a lawyer?"

"Yes, I do," she replied. "I'm going to hang up right now and call Joe Leibowitz. He's the best divorce attorney you've never heard of, and he likes it that way. You don't want to hire someone who likes to see his name in the paper. This needs to be kept very quiet, at least for now. Okay, Emma? Call me back in fifteen minutes and in the meantime you print out every one of those emails. Do it now."

Obediently, mindlessly, I went back to Garrett's desk and started printing the emails. As I sat there listening to the hum of the printer, inking out the words one page after another, I wanted to believe it was all a mistake.

Once I had the stack in front of me I walked back into our bedroom and looked at Garrett sleeping peacefully, his hand resting on my pillow. Then I saw the tea set he had brought me from London, still nestled in the box. Had he bought it for me before or after he'd slept with Lily?

That's when I decided. I had to confront him. I hated ignoring Riley's advice, but I wasn't as good an actor as Garrett. I needed to see his face when I showed him the emails. His reaction in that split second would tell me everything I needed to know about him—about the kind of man he really was. That's the only way I would know the truth. He would either try to come up with some kind of excuse or he would confess the truth. And if he opted to be honest, maybe, just maybe, we could recover from that.

My eyes were dry and red, and I felt shaky from sleeplessness. I went into the kitchen and sat at the counter without turning on the lights, the stack of emails in front of me. After about a half hour, one of the housekeepers came in with a bag of croissants from Balthazar and all the newspapers and flicked on the light. "Oh, Mrs. Walker," she said, startled. "I'm so sorry, I would have come in earlier if I knew you had an early start today."

"If you could just make the coffee and set up breakfast and the papers, you can take the rest of the day off," I replied, my voice devoid of emotion. "In fact, you can tell everyone to take off the rest of the day, please."

I sat there in silence as she measured the coffee and added the water. With a feeling of complete unreality, I listened to the coffeepot percolate, punctuated by puffs of steam. The housekeeper arranged the croissants on a silver platter, alongside a generous pat of butter sprinkled with sea salt, and a pot of strawberry jam from Ladurée in Paris. I had bought their jam for the first time when we were there on our honeymoon, because I liked the pale green label so much. She poured the coffee into a silver carafe and sealed the lid, then steamed milk for a small silver pitcher and placed brown sugar cubes into a silver dish with tongs. At the table in the breakfast nook, place mats and cloth napkins were set with silverware and Hermès china in the Rythme pattern in the same green as the Ladurée label. A large white bowl filled with raspberries, blueberries, and blackberries was placed in the middle.

It was all so perfect.

I heard the door of the service entrance close behind her and the key turn in the lock.

I poured my coffee and stirred in the hot milk. I thought about the first time Garrett took me to Paris and I ordered coffee from room service at the George V. "Café au lait?" the Frenchwoman had asked me in her beautiful accent over the phone. "Oui," I had replied, feeling so sophisticated. I loved the grand gesture of something so simple as coffee being served in such an elegant manner, and I vowed to make a production of it every morning.

I must have sat there in my kitchen that way for at least an hour, staring at all of the beautiful things in our apartment—all handpicked and meaningful in some way, each object with a different memory attached. Then I'd look down at the stack of emails, and then back again at our home—our home that could never, ever possibly feel the same way to me again. I could hear the water running through the pipes upstairs. Garrett was awake. My stomach flipped and I felt dizzy. He would be coming downstairs soon. He was up there, probably thinking he was going to come down here and we'd happily rehash last night's ball, talk about whom we saw and whose dresses we liked best while we read Page Six and drank coffee. The mornings were always our favorite time together.

Garrett came bounding down the steps and into the kitchen. He smelled of soap, his hair still wet from the shower, and he was wearing a black T-shirt and black sweatpants. "Good morning, my angel," he said, chipper as ever. "I didn't even hear you get up."

I turned around on the stool to face him.

"Honey, are you okay?" he said. "Are you hungover? You look awful."

Without saying a word, I picked up the stack of emails and stretched out my arm to hand them over to him.

As his eyes scanned the pages, his jaw clenched and a vein in his forehead started to show. I saw him try to compose himself, as if he were readying himself for a part. "What the fuck is this?"

"You tell me," I said, my voice squeaking out like a mouse.

"Where did you get these?"

He was stalling for time, and we both knew it. I just looked at him. Then he changed tactics. He sat down on the stool next to me. "Emma, honey, I wanted to tell you last night, but I didn't know how. Lily started emailing me when I was in London. Then she said she wanted to meet up. So I took her out to dinner because she's your friend. That's it. You should be thanking me. Do you think I wanted to spend one of my precious free evenings taking your college roommate out to dinner?"

"That's it, huh?" I said, emotionless.

"Yes, honey, yes. I love you. You know that. Jesus Christ, I don't even like Lily. I've always thought she was kind of a pain in the ass." He laughed, like we were already past it.

I reached over and pulled one of the emails out of the stack, and I read from it. " 'Lying in bed . . . can't stop thinking about you . . . your kiss, your touch . . . you drove me crazy.' " Then I looked at Garrett. "You still think she's a pain in the ass?"

"She's lying. Nothing happened." Garrett's voice was clipped and aggressive. God, how stupid did he think I was? Lily was a lot of things, but delusional wasn't one of them.

"No, Garrett, *you're* lying. You're lying through your teeth. I guess that's what I get for marrying an actor, huh?" My voice was cutting, and I wanted to hurt him with it. "I saw you. I saw you together in the auditorium last night. You can stop acting now."

Garrett stood up so fast he sent the stool crashing behind him. "Emma, I swear to God, you do not know how lucky you have it. I am a prince to you, and you don't even get it. Do you know what kind of humiliation half the women in Hollywood have to put up with?" Once again he was dancing around the truth, hoping I wouldn't notice, and he was getting more aggressive and confident with every word.

"Garrett, did you sleep with Lily?"

He let out a huff of air like he couldn't believe I was immune to his speech, and then his eyes narrowed and hardened. "You want the truth, Emma? I did. Because your bitch of a girlfriend showed up at my door wearing a trench coat and nothing on underneath. And I was lonely. Because my *wife* had better things to do than to be with me."

"So it's my fault?" I said. I started to cry, at just the moment when I wanted to be strongest.

"Yeah. You know what? It is. And the only mistake I made was sleeping with Lily. I should have just screwed some sweet little PA, like I usually do. They know how to keep their mouths shut." Then Garrett walked out of the room. I heard his footsteps hard down the hallway, and the elevator doors close behind him.

~~~~

After Garrett left, I sat in the kitchen in a daze for hours. I looked out the window, watching the sunlight as it shifted to the west. The phone rang several times, on and on, with no one here to answer it.

Finally, I got up and went upstairs to my office. I turned on my computer. Eighty-four emails.

There were a dozen or so from Riley. One from Harvey. A few from Grace. And one with all exclamation points in the subject line—clearly from Michael.

I caught a glimpse of myself in the gold, eighteenth-century rococo mirror hanging to the left of my desk. Garrett had bought it for me at a flea market on our honeymoon. I looked like hell.

I went to the bathroom and turned on the water in the shower as hot as it would go. I looked to the other side of the vast bathroom and saw Garrett's tuxedo from the night before in a heap on the floor. I wondered if it smelled like perfume, if after we parted ways last night, Lily had unfastened each of the buttons, had wrapped her arms around his bare chest and kissed his neck, just the way he liked. If he had gone down on her the way he did to me.

I got in the shower and let the hot water pour over me, burning my numbed skin, as I watched it turn bright red and splotchy. I wanted it all to be a bad dream. I wanted to wake up from this nightmare.

I kept thinking about my mom, trying to imagine how she managed to keep it together for my sister and me after my dad left. I never saw my mom cry, but I'd hear her at night sometimes. She was always as strong as a rock for us, and she never remarried. I don't think she ever trusted a man again after what happened with my dad. And I wondered if I would end up the same way.

I pulled a comb through my wet hair. My muscles ached, and my head throbbed as if I had the flu. I thought about calling Riley, but I didn't have the strength to talk to her. I didn't want to have to explain how I was feeling, maybe because I didn't even know how to identify this feeling.

I rifled through the medicine cabinet and found some Ambien that I saved for overnight flights and took one. I went into the bedroom and pulled the curtains closed. Then I reached for my iPhone one last time. There was a message I had to send before I surrendered to unconsciousness.

Lily,

Just so you know, I know. And you weren't the only one he was screwing on the side. Don't ever speak to me again.

Emma

I turned off my cell and unplugged the landline phone. The evening sun was just beginning to set and a hint of daylight was still coming through the cracks, so I got into bed and put on a sleeping mask and earplugs. I wanted to fall into a coma and forget today ever existed.

Fourteen hours later, I woke to the muffled sound of Grace's voice in the hallway. I was still in a sleep haze and wasn't sure if I was dreaming or awake. She tapped gently on the door before opening it and gingerly calling out, "Emma, are you alive?"

Her voice was muffled, as if underwater. I rolled over, propping myself up on one elbow, as I lifted the eye mask above one eye and plucked out my earplugs. "What day is it?" I asked, disoriented.

"Oh my God," she said. "What is wrong with you? Do you have the flu? I've been trying to reach you for twenty-four hours. You missed your workout this morning and you were supposed to be at a dentist's appointment afterward. And where is Garrett? You're looking at me like I have five heads. What's going on?"

"Garrett left and I don't want to talk about it," I said in a voice just above a whisper and laid my head back down on the pillow. "Can you get me my laptop? It's in my office."

I didn't have to look up to see Grace's expression. I'd known her long enough to know what she was thinking without even looking at her face. I knew she was shocked and I knew she wanted to ask me questions, but she also knew me well enough to know I didn't want to answer any of them.

A couple of minutes later, she reappeared. "I'll cancel the rest of your day," she said as she set my laptop on the nightstand. "I think I'll work in the office downstairs today, in case you need me."

I kept my eyes closed as she spoke. I didn't want to make eye contact with her because I knew I'd just start crying and I was afraid if I started, I'd never stop. When I heard the door close behind her, I turned on my computer and waited for it to load. I opened my email account and saw one from Garrett:

Emma, I love you. Don't turn your back on our marriage.

I laid my head back down on the pillow. It wasn't just that he'd cheated on me. That alone would have been incredibly hurtful, but I could have gotten over it. And it wasn't even that he'd slept with Lily. That was horrendous, obviously, but I honestly believed our marriage could have survived even that. No, it was what I saw in his face when I confronted him in the kitchen. That was what killed me, and that was what I couldn't imagine getting over. Ever. It was watching those calculating wheels turn in his head, and the face he put on to play the part of the wronged, misunderstood spouse. And it was the callous way he told me about all the others. As soon as he said it, I knew he wasn't just trying to hurt me. I knew it was true. He was just doing what they all did, screwing a few PAs on the side. No big deal, it meant nothing, he'd probably say. But it was a big deal to me. It was everything to me.

I clicked back to Garrett's email and replied:

What marriage?

I got up and went into the bathroom. My pajamas were damp with sweat and even with fourteen hours of sleep, there were dark half moons under my eyes. I had a pimple that felt like a second chin forming just beneath the surface and my hair was simultaneously flat and tangled. No wonder Garrett wanted to be with other women. Why did I ever believe that I would be enough for him?

What was I going to tell my mom? I felt such shame. I wondered where Garrett was, whom he was with, and what he would tell people. Actors have a great way of being able to turn situations in their favor, of knowing how to play their cards just right for the audience. Just look at Angelina Jolie. It was a skill, and I'd watched Garrett do it before.

My head swam. I turned off the lights and went back to bed. The longer I slept, the longer I could put off dealing with all of this.

I'd slept another two hours when the intercom buzzed. "Mrs. Walker, Mrs. Schwartz is here to see you."

"Send her up please," I responded.

A few minutes later, Riley cracked open the door. "Emma?" she whispered. "Are you awake?"

"Yes, I'm just pretending not to be."

She flipped on the lamp on the night table and looked startled by my appearance.

"Good God, Emma," she said. "You look awful." Riley was always a straight shooter. "Why didn't you call me back? Joe Leibowitz's office is ready to squeeze you in. You just need to say the word." She sat down on the edge of the bed. "Honey, talk to me. You're starting to scare me."

"I confronted Garrett with the emails," I said. Riley's eyes bulged but she restrained her urge to speak. "I'm sorry, Riley, I just had to. I had to see if there was some explanation."

"And?" she asked.

"He tried to deny it, but when I showed him the proof, he got angry and said it was my fault because I didn't go with him to London. He said his only mistake was sleeping with Lily and not a PA. He said that's what he usually does."

"Bastard." Riley shook her head with disgust. "Trying to make you believe it's your fault. I know you don't want to think about it, but you really do need a divorce attorney. You need to be ready."

I picked up my laptop so that I could avoid Riley's well-meaning laser vision. There was a new email from Garrett. The subject line was "Arrangements."

Emma—

Since your email indicates to me that you hold out no hope whatsoever of preserving our relationship, I think it is important that we recognize some issues that have to be dealt with.

You will now need to be represented by an independent attorney. Please arrange to do this immediately, as my attorneys cannot properly represent both of us in this situation. You will also need to have your current business and personal financial records transferred to a different accounting firm for the same reason.

I will no longer be responsible for debts incurred by you. I will no longer pay your personal credit card charges. I will no longer pay for your retail charge accounts. You will no longer have access to my bank accounts. You will no longer be able to use my name or to use any of my assets as collateral to arrange loans or credit—except, of course, for your half ownership of the apartment—and then only with my consent. You will no longer be covered by my insurance company. You will no longer be protected by my family medical insurance plan. You will no longer be a beneficiary of any inheritance stipulated in my will.

I also hope that any statement regarding our impending breakup will be mutually approved and simultaneously released by our respective publicists (assuming you will hire one) at an agreed-upon, appropriate time. I am not going to comment on this to anyone in the media—ever. Of course, you may do whatever you wish. I only ask that you consider and respect our seven years together whenever you are asked to talk about me or our relationship.

We are now in different camps.

—Garrett

I couldn't bear to read the email out loud to Riley, so without saying a word, I handed the laptop over to her. I watched her face as she read it.

Riley betrayed no emotions. She set down the computer, picked up her cell phone, and said, "It's go time."

## 12

"For the love of God," Michael exclaimed as he walked into the living room. "*That* was an experience—not one I care to repeat, either. Those paparazzi are animals," he continued. "Special, I tell you, real special."

I smirked. "You're looking especially dapper today. Almost like you knew you'd be photographed." Within twenty-four hours of Garrett's last email to me, his publicist, Alex—formerly *our* publicist, Alex—had prepared a statement for the press. It said that we had mutually agreed to separate. Then all hell broke loose, and my apartment building had been surrounded ever since.

Michael didn't dignify my comment with a response, but even for him, a perfectly tailored Dior suit and Gucci loafers wasn't exactly errand-running attire. "You have to admit, although it completely sucks, it is kind of glamorous. I keep imagining you going down there in a full-length fur, turban, and gigantic Chanel sunglasses, with red lipstick, smoking a cigarette, and telling them all to drop dead." Michael walked over to the bar and started to mix himself a drink, filling the shaker with ice, topping it with gin and vermouth. I watched him shake the cocktail and pour the chilled liquid into a vintage martini glass, topping it with a single olive.

"You look like a gay Don Draper," I said.

"I do?" he asked, clearly delighted. "That's exactly what I was going for."

He handed me the martini and then made one for himself. The icy gin slid soothingly down my throat and I chewed on a salty olive while Michael told me about the shoot he was putting together in Patagonia. He was talking to me as if nothing had happened, knowing that I was sick to death of my own problems. I felt like I was a patient in a hospital with a terminal disease and my friends were coming in shifts to visit me. Their attempts didn't really take my mind off my slow and painful death, but I appreciated their efforts, nonetheless. Michael froze up in the face of real emotion, but he was a master of the art of distraction. I half listened as he described styling the U.S. women's Olympic snowboarding team's couture on a mountaintop.

After he'd drained two drinks in the time it took me to finish one, he got up to leave for a fashion industry cocktail party that I would have been attending as well if not for my situation. I walked him to the front door and he took me in his long arms and wrapped me in a bear hug. He pulled back and looked down at me through his thick black-rimmed glasses.

"Emma, all the ridiculous fashion talk aside," he said in a serious tone, "you need to get out of here. You've been in this apartment for a week and you can't stay cooped up forever. Go be anonymous somewhere until it all blows over." He gave me one last squeeze and was out the door.

The idea of leaving my apartment was both exhilarating and terrifying. I felt like I was in my own little cocoon in here, and I'd started to develop a bunker mentality. It was me or the paparazzi, and I'd be damned if I let them win.

But watching Michael escape from my apartment like a parolee, I realized that my forced imprisonment was a no-win scenario. I had a little buzz going from the martini and my mind started to wander off to where I'd like to go, if I could leave. I didn't want to go to Paris—too many memories. The same was true for St. Barts. The tabloids were even more ravenous in England and Australia, so scratch those places. L.A. and the Hamptons were no different than New York, and both were filled with familiar faces and endless gossip. I wanted to be somewhere warm. Somewhere with a beach. Somewhere that I could wear a caftan and eat. Somewhere no one knew me.

Mexico?

Garrett would never go to Mexico. He wouldn't even go to a Mexican restaurant with me. He called it "poor people's leftovers." ("Why would anyone want *re*fried beans?" he'd always ask when I suggested it.) So I only ate Mexican when Garrett was out of town—it was my single-girl food. And now I was a single girl again.

My liquid courage took me over to the elevator and up to my office. I clicked on Google and resisted the urge to type in my own name. Instead I searched "sleepy beach towns in Mexico."

Every search led me back to Sayulita. I ignored the pictures of young couples in love and focused instead on the deep blue ocean and lava formations that made it look remote and untouched. Just what I wanted—just what I needed.

I called Grace and told her my plan. She was all for it, and suggested that we charter a plane in her name instead of mine. She didn't even trust one of our drivers or a car service, and said that she'd take me to the airport herself. But how would I get out of the apartment without being seen and followed? "The service entrance—preferably after midnight," Grace said. "That's how."

I felt a sense of lightness for the first time in a week, and I decided to pack with the same attitude. During my years with Garrett, I usually sent my luggage ahead wherever we traveled—a large Louis Vuitton trunk filled with clothes, jewelry, shoes, and bags. I thought back to that first trip to St. Barts and what I'd packed then—I was naïve enough to think that a beach vacation meant that you didn't need much more than a bikini, a pair of shorts, and flip-flops. I wasn't that girl anymore, but I could at least try to pack like her. Into my suitcase went a few cotton tunics that I'd picked up in a market in India, my favorite jeans, a couple of bikinis, a straw hat, some shorts, and flip-flops. I almost reached for a dress and a pair of heels and then I thought, Screw it. I hate heels. There, I said it. *I hate heels.*

I put on a pair of black yoga pants, a black tank, and a black hooded zip-up jacket, and at exactly midnight I went out the service exit to the back staircase of the building, carrying only my purse. I opened the back door and stepped into the alley, and realized it was the first time I'd been outside in a week—no, make that eight days. The air felt damp and cool. I paused to take a deep breath, and then gagged on the smell of trash. I must have startled a rat, and it darted under the Dumpster. Ah, the glamour of New York. Quickening my pace to a near sprint, I reached the end of the alley just as Grace pulled up. I got in the passenger seat and we were off, piece of cake.

After the initial exhilaration, though, I suddenly felt deeply sad. My war against the paparazzi had been a distraction from the bitter truth that my life would never, ever be the same again. My husband had cheated on me with one of my oldest friends, my marriage was over, and I didn't even know if I'd have a home to come back to. Garrett and I may have been growing apart the last few years—and I'd had a lot of time in the last week to ponder that—but still, he was my husband. And I'd taken for granted that he was there for me, that I was part of a team. He was the last call I made when I got on an airplane, and the first call I made when I got off—I had no one to call now.

"Hey you, are you all right?" Grace reached over and squeezed my knee. "I'm glad you're doing this, you know?"

"Me too. I'm just sad," I said. I would have sworn to anyone that I hadn't thought twice about Lily in the last week, but I guess I was lying to myself and everyone else. "Any news from Lily?"

Grace looked surprised. "God, how the hell would I know? It's not like we've ever been friends. You know I only put up with her for your sake."

"Well, you had better sense than I did. I should have known she was bad news from the day I met her. How could I ever have thought she loved me? She only loves herself." My cheeks burned with the shame of Garrett's parting words—that it was my fault that he'd had sex with her. "Do you know that she's never even called me to apologize?"

Grace shook her head. "Look, she's a coward not to call you, and I have no respect for her. But I feel sorry for her."

"Why? She got what she wanted, right? Why feel sorry for *her*?"

"Garrett's not going to leave his wife for her best friend. That's not his style. So all Lily got out of this is a bad reputation. And she lost you in the process. That's a lose-lose," Grace said.

"So why'd she do it, Grace? I mean . . . how could she?" I'd been so angry at Lily when it happened, and so focused on my grief over Garrett, that it wasn't until this moment that I admitted to myself how brokenhearted I was to be betrayed by a friend.

"Because she's desperate."

I huffed a laugh. "To have sex with my husband?"

"That's not what I mean. She's desperate to be taken care of. And she's scared. She's not married, her career is stalled. She's no Diane Keaton. What's she going to do in ten, twenty years when the young, cute girl parts dry up? It's scary out there, Emma."

She didn't have to remind me how scary it was out there. I remember the relief I felt when I married Garrett and no longer had to worry about paying the rent. The sudden relaxation in my chest when losing my scholarship became a lighthearted joke instead of a defining, life-changing humiliation. All the luxury of my life with Garrett was new to me, and I appreciated every second of it—the doors he opened for me, the meetings he arranged, the bills he paid. Now it was just my life. Nothing special, really. I didn't even notice it anymore. Sure, I'd worked hard on my script, and thanks to its success, a lot of people in Hollywood made a lot of money. I was proud of that. But would that movie ever have been made if I hadn't been married to Garrett?

"That was me, too, Grace," I said.

Grace looked at me quizzically.

"I was scared, too," I said. "I wanted to be taken care of, too."

Grace nodded, "Well, who wouldn't?"

"You, Grace. You're not looking to have anyone else take care of you. What makes you so strong?"

"Oh God, Emma. Everyone wants to be taken care of. I'm no different." She shrugged. "Pete would have taken care of me. But I guess I just felt like that wasn't enough, you know?"

I nodded. "I know. It's not enough for me anymore, either."

~~~~~~~~

I'd been in the casita at the resort for three days, but I hadn't even unpacked. There was a large living room, dining room, kitchen, and bedroom. It even had its own swimming pool and steps leading down to the beach. But I barely took it in. I thought that the closer I got to Mexico, the happier—the more free—I'd feel. Instead I looked out at the ocean right outside my window, and I felt lost.

So I drew the shades, and I went to sleep. I kept the DO NOT DISTURB sign on my door and only removed it when I ordered room service. The waiter would wheel in the cart while I stayed hidden in my bedroom, and I'd come out only after I heard the door close behind him.

Sometimes I woke up and forgot where I was, and for just a brief moment, I'd feel okay—like it was all just a bad dream. Other times I woke up in a pool of sweat, terrified that my life was over. I'd lost my husband, and with him I would lose everything else—my career, my home, my status. I'd go back to being Emma Guthrie—a poor girl from Kentucky who didn't quite fit in anywhere, struggling to get by. The worst times were when I rolled over and instinctively reached out my hand for Garrett—to gently tug on the hairs of his chest absentmindedly, to press my body up against his purposefully—and then realized he wasn't there. He had become my phantom limb, and I felt just as empty and grief-stricken as if I'd truly lost a part of me. I had loved that man—so much. And I would never touch him again. Those were the times I cried.

Finally, my body rebelled and refused to sleep anymore. I glanced at the clock—5:18 a.m. I went into the bathroom and flipped on the light, my eyes burning as they adjusted to the brightness. I looked like shit—my skin was oily and my hair was dull and matted to my head. Showering hadn't been at the top of my priority list the last few days. It was time, to say the least.

The soap felt good on my skin. As I massaged the shampoo on my scalp, rubbing my aching temples, I thought back to the first time I saw *South Pacific* when I was about ten years old. My mom had rented it for a sleepover and for days, Grace and I danced around the house singing "I'm gonna wash that man right outta my hair." If only it were that easy.

I dug through my suitcase and pulled out a caftan. Showered and dressed, this was real progress. I went in the kitchen, brewed a pot of coffee, and filled a mug. The smell roused my senses and I took my coffee out to the patio and curled up on a lounge chair.

It was still dark. The air was warm and humid. My mind was blissfully blank as I listened to the waves beat against the shore and watched the sky lighten from deep purple to lavender. Soon a series of black dots emerged on the water. Every so often, a wave rolled in and one of the dots moved to shore. As it got brighter, I realized those dots weren't some kind of weird Mexican sea life, they were surfers. I propped myself up and watched as one after another took turns riding a wave to shore and then paddled back out. God, they looked so graceful. How were they not afraid?

The ocean had always terrified me. I'd never gone in over my head—and usually not past my knees. The force of the waves always scared me, and I had an unhealthy fear of everything that lurked beneath. I was even afraid of seaweed. But those surfers looked fearless.

I watched them for a few hours, mesmerized by the way they'd take a wave with such confidence, twisting and turning their bodies, going up and down the face of the waves, the white water spraying up around the surfboard. One by one, as the sun got higher in the sky, the surfers each rode a wave to shore and came out of the water, effortlessly carrying their boards under one arm.

Once they were all gone and were slowly replaced by tourists, I grew tired and went back into my bedroom. I got into bed and tried to sleep, but it was no good. I looked over at my computer and unconsciously twisted one of my earrings. I had told myself that I would use my laptop only for working on the screenplay, not for surfing the Web to find out what was being said about me, and not even for emailing. There wasn't anyone in New York or anywhere else who couldn't wait to talk to me. I'd spoken to my mother before I left, and if she got really worried about me she knew where to find me. Michael would do just fine without me to fuss over for a little while. I even thought about contacting Riley, bless her, but I changed my mind when I realized that she would just nag me about talking to a lawyer, and the very thought of it made me ill. Momentarily I considered checking in with Grace. Wanting to spare me from even having to log into email, she had promised to call the hotel if there were any genuine emergencies. I threw a pillow onto the computer and turned away. Reality could wait.

Or so I thought. I flipped on the TV and scrolled through pay-per-view. And there it was, my movie. It wasn't reality, but it was as close to it as a Hollywood romance could get. I had spent years bringing my love story with Garrett to film, and now here I was lying in bed in Mexico, and it was all over—the love story and the marriage that followed it. All I had ever wanted was for people to watch my movie, and now I wished no one would see it or hear of it ever again.

I turned off the TV, tightly closed the curtains, made sure that the DO NOT DISTURB sign was in place, and took an Ambien with a shot of tequila from the minibar.

~~~~~

The clock glared at me: 3:24 a.m.

I pressed my eyes closed, trying my best to will myself back to sleep. I felt groggy and dizzy from my Ambien cocktail the day before. If I wasn't asleep by 5 a.m., I told myself, I'd get up and watch those surfers again.

I kept peeking at the clock—4:08 a.m. Then 4:52 a.m. I stayed still until 5:05 a.m. Then I went outside and scanned the horizon. Nothing yet, it was still too dark. Finally, as the sun began to rise, it illuminated the water with an iridescent glow that was magical. And there were the little black dots, floating in the water. I was transfixed.

As if those surfers were calling to me, I went back in and pulled on shorts, then took the steps down to the beach. The instant my feet hit the sand, I felt some solace. I walked into the surf and stood there up to my ankles, then I planted myself in the sand and once again I watched for hours. Just like yesterday, once day had fully broken, one by one the surfers left the water with their boards. Some of them looked like they could put on a business suit and walk into an office without causing an eyebrow to lift. Others looked like they might live in a cardboard box somewhere.

Eventually only one surfer remained out in the water, looking toward the horizon, awaiting his next wave. I watched his long, lean silhouette stand up on the board and ride the wave as if there were no disconnect between him and the board. He looked so at ease, as if there were no place else he wanted to be and nothing else on his mind but the surf. I wanted to feel that way.

He came to shore, then emerged from the water. Tall, shaggy blond hair, tan. Utterly, breathtakingly beautiful. He left the beach, never looking back.

I watched him walk away, my mouth open, and then I looked back at the water. I got to my feet and walked in. Step by step. Past my ankles, then my knees. Past my thighs, then my crotch. Then my waist. I felt the pull of the surf, out and in, and the waves started to threaten in a way they didn't when I was safely onshore. I was terrified, but I forced myself to stand there, two seconds, five seconds, and then I ran to shore, gasping and stumbling.

I couldn't remember ever feeling like that. It felt completely unsafe, and everything in that murky water still terrified me, but there was something else, too. Excitement, and . . . nerve. I had felt brave, for just a few seconds. And when I was out there, the surf spraying into my nostrils, I wasn't thinking of anything else but staying on my feet.

Before I could talk myself out of it, I marched back up the steps and into my casita. I ripped off my wet clothes and changed into a dry bikini and shorts. Then I went straight to the hotel lobby.

There was a nice-looking young man at the front desk whose name tag read "Pablo."

"Buenos dias, how may I help you?" he asked politely.

"Buenos dias, I'd like to schedule a surfing lesson," I said.

"Very good, señora. I know of an excellent instructor," he said. "When would you like a lesson?"

"Now," I said. "I mean, as soon as possible. Today, please."

"Not a problem. I will ring your room as soon as I have a time scheduled for you."

"Actually, I'll just wait here in the lobby until he comes." I knew that if I went back to my room there was a very strong chance that I'd get into bed again, and Pablo's phone call would go unanswered.

"As you wish, señora."

I sat, and then I paced, then I had a coffee. Finally, Pablo tapped me on the shoulder.

"Señora, your surfing instructor has arrived," he said.

I turned, and there he was: Tall, shaggy blond hair, tan. Utterly, breathtakingly beautiful.

And for the first time in exactly twelve days, I realized that I was looking forward to something.

## 13

His name was Ben, and I followed him in silence down to the beach. He carried his surfboard over his head and wore a pale blue T-shirt, damp with sweat and stained with zinc around the collar, and white board shorts with navy stripes. His shoulders were broad, the T-shirt clinging to ripples of muscle down his back and the sleeves tight around his biceps. His skin was tanned to a golden bronze, and his hair was windblown and the color of sand.

As I walked behind him, noticing every detail of his body and the easy way he carried himself, I felt a queasy flip-flop in my belly that I hadn't felt for another man since I'd met Garrett. *Calm yourself, Emma.* I distracted myself by focusing instead on the ragged little black and tan mutt who followed every step that Ben took. When we got to the beach I leaned down to pet the dog and soon he was on his back, all four feet in the air and begging for a belly scratch.

"Sweet dog," I said. "What's his name?"

"Fernando. He followed me home from town one day, and I haven't been able to shake him." Ben laid his surfboard in the sand and then leaned over and gave the dog an affectionate push. "All right, Fernando. Get lost now. Unless you're going to teach the girl to surf."

Fernando rolled in the sand and found a good spot for a nap. Ben laughed. "Yeah, I didn't think so. Okay, Emma, this is your first time surfing, yeah? What made you want to give it a shot?"

"Not really sure," I answered. "I've always been kind of afraid of the ocean, and I'm not very athletic or coordinated, so this could be a disaster."

"I'll take it easy on you, at least for today," he said. "Let's work on getting you comfortable on the board and in the water. You might stand up today, you might not. The most important thing to do is to stay relaxed and never panic—that's when you get in trouble."

Hmm. Words to live by.

I slipped off my shorts, ready to get in the water.

"We're actually going to start right here," he said. "On the sand. I want you to try a few pop-ups before we get in the water."

Ben proceeded to demonstrate a pop-up—and it looked simultaneously easy and impossible. He lay down on the board, paddling, then gracefully arched his body, quickly pulled his feet up under him and popped up into a surfing stance, his knees soft and his body in perfect balance. It took him a matter of seconds.

I watched him and thought, Oh my God, why didn't I keep my shorts on? He traded places with me and I lay down on the board feeling ten different kinds of stupid while I paddled in the sand. The worst part was still to come, because then I had to stick my butt up in the air to imitate that lunge position—in a *bikini*, let's not forget. Then I pulled my feet under me and popped up, praying for dear life that I wouldn't fall. I didn't, but I felt like a total jackass. What on earth made me think I could do this? If I was this pathetic on land, what the hell was I going to be like in the water? And why was I paying good money to look and feel this foolish?

"Okay," Ben said. "I think you're ready to get in the water."

Really?

He pulled his T-shirt over his head, and it was as if the clouds parted and a heavenly chorus burst into song. God, he was spectacular. Washboard abs, and just a spray of hair on his chest, bleached almost white from the sun.

"Wear my T-shirt," he said. "You'll want to get a rash guard before our next lesson. I can set you up with that."

A rash guard? I didn't like the sound of that. Exactly what kind of rash was I guarding against? But I chose not to ask questions. I wanted to play it cool, even though I had no clue what he was talking about.

He strapped the surfboard leash to my ankle and carried the board as we walked down to the ocean together. We waded mid-thigh into the water, and he told me to hop on the board.

"Slide up. I'm going to get on here with you and paddle you out," he said.

I obliged, and I felt him slide onto the board, his face pretty much level with my butt. As if I hadn't been self-conscious enough already.

"Come back a little bit more," he said, grabbing my legs and pulling me back a few inches before I could respond.

"Perfect, let's go," he said, and started to paddle me out into the water.

This wasn't so bad. He was doing all the work and I was along for the ride. But that little vacation was short-lived. When we got out past the point where the waves were breaking, Ben slid off the board and swam around to face me. His eyes were so blue that they were startling, but his face was gentle, and his voice was patient and encouraging, and I found that he had a bizarrely calming effect on me.

"When a wave comes, I'm going to push you into it and you're going to paddle as hard as you can," he said. "When you hear me yell 'pop up,' you're going to do exactly what you did on the sand. You'll be able to feel it—the wave will start to carry you, and that's when you'll jump up. When you fall, just make sure you cover your head when you come up so you don't get hit in the face with the board."

Okay, that wasn't so calming.

"And if you get in trouble," he continued, "I'm right here and I'll come and get you. Just relax and have fun. You ready?"

Before I could answer, he was pushing me, I was paddling, and then I heard his command to pop up. I got my feet under my body but fell backward immediately, instinctively resisting the forward pull of the board and the wave. I sucked water in through my nose as I felt the wave turn me upside down and sideways. But I wasn't afraid. There was something comforting about that leash around my ankle, tied to this floating thing above me. I grabbed hold of the board and pulled myself up to the surface, as if my body knew what to do even if my mind didn't. Then another wave came down on top of me and the process repeated all over again, like I was a pair of jeans in a washing machine. I got up and back onto the board that time, and paddled myself back out to Ben.

As I got closer to him I saw that he had a big grin on his face. He shouted, "You got hammered! Nice!" and then gave me a big high five when I reached him.

Even though my sinuses were burning, and I was pretty sure snot was running down to my chin, I didn't even flinch when he said it was time to do it again. And again.

Before I knew it, class was over. "See ya tomorrow, surfer girl. I'll bring you a rash guard."

I swear, if he'd patted me on the head and given me a cookie, I couldn't have felt prouder of myself.

Every day I had a lesson, and I got a little bit better. Then I spent the rest of the day reading and swimming. I'd started to eat again, too, and I found that whatever I ate after I surfed tasted incredibly good.

By day four, I could stand up on the board, but I still couldn't ride the wave. I'd get up on the board and immediately get hammered by a wave, or three. Then I'd paddle back to Ben and he'd push me back out again. And that's how we spent two hours, every day.

Ben was unlike anyone I'd ever met before. If I'd counted, everything he said might have added up to twenty words. But his effect on me was like a serenity injection. I just didn't worry about anything when I was around him. It must have been something to do with the state of mind that resulted from a whole lifetime spent surfing. His only concern in life was finding the next wave. He had not a thing else to worry about, so he became a human-shaped ocean of calm.

"Change of plans today," he said as I arrived for my fifth lesson.

"Are we not surfing?" My face fell.

"Oh no, we're surfing," he said. "Just not here. You're gonna ride a wave today, no doubt. I'm taking you somewhere special—you're gonna like it."

I followed Ben and Fernando up the trail past the resort and into the employee parking lot. I spotted his car before he even pointed it out to me. It was exactly what I'd pictured he'd drive—a beat-up old Jeep, the paint peeling and patched with rust, a pile of surfboards sticking out the back. He jerked the passenger door open, using some force, and I climbed up into the seat. Fernando clambered into the backseat and found a spot amid the damp towels, fishing rods, and gas can. Even though it was open air, there was a whiff of mildew and the floor was covered in sand. Ben went around to the driver's side and jumped in, then reached across me to yank my door closed. His arm, the hair bleached from the sun, brushed across me. I felt a quiver of excitement, and I realized that I was actually holding my breath. I thought I'd gotten past this over the last few days, but obviously not. *Breathe, Emma. And get a grip while you're at it. He's your surfing instructor. End of story.*

After shaking some sense into myself, I began to enjoy the ride—my first time outside the gates of the resort. The wind felt good whipping my hair around my face, and occasionally I stole a glance over at Ben. His crow's feet were thin white lines where he squinted in the sun, and I wondered how old he could be. He might be my age, or much older. It was impossible to tell.

We rode along in silence, but it wasn't awkward, because he was clearly so content with the quiet, and I didn't feel the need to fill the air with chatter. We drove through the hippie surf town of Sayulita—tiny, and lined with surf shops and bare-bones outdoor eateries. Locals and their children milled around alongside surfers of every age and nationality. Then we turned onto a dirt road at a small cemetery, the graves decorated with brightly colored flowers and streamers, and up a hill that led us into the jungle.

"We're almost there," Ben said.

As we neared the top of the hill, it felt like the Jeep could topple over at any moment. The old Emma in me would have gripped the dashboard and told him to be careful, but my inner nag was silent—Ben had that effect on me. He took a turn around a bend at the top and paradise was below. He put the Jeep in park and leaned over me again to open my door.

Fernando raced out ahead of us, and we walked down a winding path to the beach, listening to the sound of birds calling out over the rolling waves. If I ever needed inspiration for writing, this should be it. I'd never seen any place so beautiful in all my life.

The beach was completely empty—not a soul or a creature in sight, only a deserted-looking house on a cliff jutting out above. We left Fernando on the beach with our towels and paddled into the waves, side by side. I was now past the point where I needed him to paddle me out—unfortunately. Still, our time together was always very physical, but there never seemed to be anything even slightly self-conscious or sexual in the way that Ben touched me. He strapped the leash to my ankle, readjusted my position on the board, and often grabbed my hand to help me through a wave. At the beginning I'd been shocked by his physicality, but now it just felt natural. That flutter I felt in the Jeep when his arm brushed across me had passed, and we were back in the water—back to normal.

Actually, the most romantic moments out there in the ocean had nothing to do with Ben. All of the things that used to scare me the most about the sea—its depth and unknown quality—were now the things that attracted me most. It gave me a feeling of being a small piece of nature—not separate from the expanse at all, but an integral part of it. And when a wave rolled past, and the white water sprayed back, tickling my face with its drops and creating a momentary rainbow in the mist, it was almost as if I could see God, just for a split second.

"Wouldn't that be an amazing house to live in?" I said, pointing up toward the cliff. "Just give it all up and live on the beach."

"That is a cool little spot, isn't it? I've never seen anybody up there. Don't think anyone's lived there in years."

"So what is your story?" I asked. "What brought you here?"

"My dear, that is another story for another time," he said, and pushed me into a wave before I could protest his response.

After I tried my luck at a couple of waves, and each time stood up only to tumble down again, Ben told me to sit up on the board for a minute. Then he climbed up on the other end of my board and sat facing me.

"Emma," he said to me with a lighthearted tone, "you've got control issues."

He must have been able to read the stunned expression on my face pretty clearly. I was never good at hiding my emotions.

"You could surf, if you would just let go," he said. "You

keep jumping off the board. You get to your feet, and then you jump off."

"But—"

"You have to give up control," he said, looking at me intensely with his blue eyes. Oh, those blue eyes. "You aren't in charge out here, and that's a good thing. Turn yourself over to the wave and just ride it."

How had this guy figured me out already? Just by watching me fall off a few waves? I didn't know whether to laugh or cry. I'd told myself that I was ready to give in and feel unsafe for a while, but I'd still been holding out—still trying to hang on to the side of the pool where nothing bad could happen to me.

"Yeah, man, like totally," I said, feigning a California surfer dude voice. "Like, just let go, like."

"Oh, you're in for it now," he said, and flipped me off the board into the water.

I broke the surface and heard him laughing uproariously.

"You're so pleased with yourself, aren't you, Surfer?" I said, laughing, too. "So you think you've got me all psychoanalyzed? Well, we'll see about this whole control thing."

After a few more failed attempts to "turn myself over to the wave," followed by Ben yelling at me to "stop jumping off the board," the tide was starting to change and it was about time for our lesson to end.

All I wanted was to stand up on that board and ride it to shore. I could just feel that I was on the brink of doing it. And it wasn't just because I wanted to please Ben—I wanted to prove to myself that I could do it, that I could live without a safety net.

"Okay, Emma," Ben said to me in all seriousness. "This is your last shot for today. You gonna stand up for me?"

I nodded with certainty, and he pushed the board into the wave. I could do this. Mustering every ounce of confidence I had left inside, I pulled my feet under me and stood up. Oh shit—I was moving . . . fast. My first instinct was to jump off, but in those few seconds, Ben's voice was a mantra in my head— "Let go, let go, let go"—and I stayed with it. With my knees bent, my arms out to steady my balance, I rode that wave. The sensation was unlike anything I'd felt before, but I imagined the closest thing I could compare it to was flying—if I had wings and could just take off and soar around the sky, that's what it would feel like. I stayed with that wave all the way, until the water ripped my board out from under me and I fell right onto my butt in the shallow water. Normally I would have whined about the discomfort, but I was elated—no, I was euphoric. I felt high. I turned and looked at Ben, and with his hands up over his head he was throwing his fists into the air and cheering. The next wave he surfed in to meet me. He threw his arms around me and then leaned back for a high five.

"Gidget!" he exclaimed. "That was awesome!"

For all I know, we sailed back to the resort—I was so high I didn't feel like my butt was even touching the seat. When we pulled up to the gates, I was still grinning ear to ear.

"So what do you do with your days here when you're not surfing?" Ben asked as he eased the Jeep into park.

"Not a lot," I said. "I read, I do some writing. Sleep mostly. I like to be alone."

"Alone is cool." Ben nodded. "But you need to get out, experience the culture here. And you need to celebrate your first wave. I'll pick you up at eight."

~~~~~

I dug through my suitcase. Maybe I should have brought a dress with me. Instead I pulled out my favorite old jeans and a brightly colored tunic. I washed my hair and let it dry curly, and put on some silver flip-flops. I never wanted to wear high heels again. I smiled, imagining a life without sore feet.

I took one last look in the mirror, surveying my appearance, and saw that there was one thing that looked out of place here. I took off one diamond earring, then the other, put them in an envelope and marked it "For Housekeeping," and left it on my pillow.

At exactly eight o'clock, Ben's dusty Jeep pulled around the circle at the hotel entrance.

"Wow," he said. "You look pretty all dressed up."

I looked down at myself and laughed. Only Ben would think a clean tunic and jeans was dressed up. He wore a wrinkled white button-down with the sleeves rolled up, torn jeans, and flip-flops, and I guess that was dressed up for him, too.

"Not so bad yourself, Surfer," I said. "Where are you taking me?"

"You'll see, just a little local flavor," he said. "A little food, a little alcohol, maybe some dancing."

"Where's Fernando?" I asked. "I don't think I've ever seen him more than ten feet away from you when you're not in the water."

Ben smiled. "He's got a date. I gave him the night off."

We parked just outside town and then walked through the dusty cobblestone streets of Sayulita. People were out and about enjoying the slight cool of evening, shop doors were still open, and stray dogs scampered around looking for handouts. Rather than eating at a restaurant, we went from taco stand to taco stand trying each family's recipes. Ben told me what to order at each stand ("She makes the best fish tacos," and "You gotta try the tacos al pastor this guy makes"). Then we walked toward the beach to a little bar that was buzzing with a mix of locals and expats. We sat at the bar and Ben ordered us a few beers.

Once they were half drained and we'd been sitting in companionable silence for a while, I looked at Ben. "Okay, so today you said your life was another story for another time, and guess what? It's another time."

"Really? Oh man, I hate talking about myself." He bowed his head slightly and raked his fingers through his shaggy hair. I found myself wanting to bury my hands in there.

"Yes, Surfer. Inquiring minds want to know," I said. "Where did you grow up?"

"L.A."

"Did you always like surfing?"

"Pretty much."

Tough interview. I persisted. "How did you end up in Mexico?"

"I've traveled all over the place to surf," he said. "South Africa, I was in Biarritz awhile, spent some time in Puerto Rico, then I moved to Indo for a couple years, and now I'm here. Been here about two years." He called to the bartender, "Juan, how about a couple tequila shots down here?"

"Are you trying to get me drunk and take advantage of me?" I asked with a smile. Oh my God, I was flirting. I needed to be stopped.

"Welcome to Mexico," he said, then licked his wrist, sprinkled it with salt, and nodded for me to follow suit.

I did, and after the bite of salt, I shuddered and then the

warmth of the shot washed through me. It was heaven, and I felt giddy.

Ben pointed toward the beach. "The band looks like they're about to get started. Time to dance."

The dance floor was right on the sand and lit with Christmas lights strung overhead. Ben took me by the hand and led me down to the beach. We left our shoes to the side, and he pulled my arms around his neck and took me by the waist, moving me back and forth to the beat of the music. He was a great dancer, and I was . . . well, grateful for the tequila. The air was humid and the more we danced the more we sweated, the more my hair curled, and the less I cared—about anything. He picked me up, he dipped me, he twirled me around and around.

I was having so much *fun*. Fun like I hadn't had in years. Fun like fun I couldn't remember *ever* having. I felt electric when I looked at Ben. I wanted to kiss him. I wondered if he wanted to kiss me, too. Oh girl, I said to myself, this is headed nowhere good. If I had stopped right then and headed back to the resort, it would have been the safe thing to do. But I really didn't want to be safe.

We danced until the band stopped playing, well past midnight. I didn't want the night to be over, and we walked down to the ocean and let the water touch our toes.

"So I should be asking you," he said. "What brought you to Mexico?"

"Now that is definitely another story for another time." I smiled.

We looked at each other, our eyes locking for a moment longer than they should have. If he was ever going to kiss me, now would be the time.

"Well, we should be heading back," he said.

"Oh yeah, sure, I'm tired," I said, nodding in agreement (as if I wouldn't have stayed out all night if he'd only asked me).

It's for the best, I thought on the drive home. I was just getting caught up in the moment. I couldn't have a fling with my surf teacher. Please. How cliché. I involuntarily shook my head. What was I even thinking? Besides, this trip was supposed to give me time to figure myself out—this was not the time for a mindless roll in the sand with a hot guy. But, damn. He was really hot.

I took a shower before bed to cool off, but I couldn't sleep, even though I was exhausted. Hours of surfing, hours of dancing, and my muscles were crying out for mercy. But my body wouldn't relax. All I could think about was how it would feel to have Ben on top of me, kissing my neck, touching me, what sex would be like with him.

I tossed and turned, overheated even with the air conditioner on high. Finally, near daybreak, I fell asleep just as the surfers were gathering in the waves outside my casita.

## 14

The next morning I shook off the fantasy of the night before and walked down to the beach like usual, two coffees in hand (a little cream for me, black for Ben). Fernando greeted me, and I could see that Ben was still out surfing, so I sat down next to the little mutt and scratched his ears. Ben was a beautiful surfer; his movements in the water were at once languid, and playful, and elegant—he exuded pure joy. It was inspiring to watch someone who devoted his life to doing one thing extraordinarily well.

When Ben came up on the beach, he greeted me just like he did every other morning—"Hey Gidget"—and we were back to our routine of no idle chitchat and hours of surfing.

The next day we went back to the beach where I'd ridden my first wave, and I looked up at that house on the cliff.

I've never considered myself much of a spiritual person, but just sitting on my board in the water at that moment, I had such a feeling of well-being that I genuinely believed that no matter what happened in my life—good or bad or in between—it would all be okay. I could see why some surfers just never stopped surfing—they kept going and going. Just then I could have moved into that house up there and done nothing but this for the rest of my life. It was that intoxicating.

And there was something about being out there with Ben that felt just as right. I felt like I was the real me when I was with him. He put me at ease—there wasn't any part of me that I tried to hide or change for his benefit or mine. I was strong and vulnerable, confident and shy, adventurous and afraid, and somehow he seemed to know all those sides of me, and more, instinctively. And even though Ben was loath to talk about himself, I could sense he was letting me in a little more each day, giving me a chance to know him as well. He wasn't playing the part of my surfing instructor, or acting a certain way because he thought it was expected of him. He was just himself. And he was becoming a true friend to me.

Because my time with Ben was so idyllic, I should have known that it had to come to an end, but the thought hadn't even crossed my mind. Not a glimmer of reality disturbed my happy stupor. And then a storm at sea changed everything.

"You're in luck, Gidget," Ben told me as we paddled out that morning. "There's a groundswell building and you get to surf the first gentle waves of it."

"A groundswell?" I said. "That sounds kind of scary."

"Nah, just the opposite," he said. "A groundswell is the most ideal surfing condition—perfectly balanced, even waves. It's caused by a distant storm. Way out there, there's a storm in the ocean that's sending you your best surf yet."

"Cool."

"It's still small, but I'm going to leave early tomorrow morning to drive up north where it gets really big and camp out for a few days."

"Well that sucks." I had a feeling that to a surfer like Ben, a few days could mean anything.

"Ah, Gidget is upset she's not gonna get her surfing lesson," he teased. "You'll be just fine. It'll be too big tomorrow for you to surf anyway. Besides, you like being alone, remember?"

I did like to be alone, but at that moment, I realized that I preferred to be alone with Ben.

That day of surfing was my best yet. It would take years of practice before I could paddle myself into a wave, but once Ben gave me a push, I was up and riding waves all the way in, over and over. I felt like a superstar, and managed to forget for a little while that I wouldn't be able to do this again for days.

After the lesson, we were drying off on the beach and I was wondering whether a hug goodbye would be appropriate, when Ben whipped me lightly with the end of his towel. "Want to come over for lunch today?"

"You cook?" I asked, surprised.

"Yep. Actually, I speared a few pompano last night and I don't want them to go to waste while I'm away."

"Man versus Wild, I like it," I said. "I'll bring the wine."

ordered a bottle of white wine from room service and followed Ben's directions to his place—about a mile down the beach and then up a steep path. The front door was open, only covered by a curtain that looked like it was made from the fabric of an Indian sari.

"Anybody home?" I called out, peeking around the curtain. It was more of a shack than a house, but it had running water and electricity, a small bathroom with a toilet and sink, and an outdoor shower. It was as if I had conjured it from my imagination, complete with Mexican blankets, travel postcards pinned to the rough-hewn walls, and books lining one wall on homemade shelves. I caught sight of *On the Road* by Jack Kerouac. More surprising, right next to it was a well-worn copy of *Pride and Prejudice*. Interesting. What I couldn't have imagined even if I'd tried was the view out to sea. It was spectacular, and if we'd been in Malibu or the Hamptons, the property would surely have been worth millions. But here it was simply a proper spot for a humble surfer to hang his wet suit.

"I'm out back," Ben called from the other side of the house. I walked around and saw him standing at the grill with Fernando by his side, sitting at attention as he waited for a bite to fall his way. The grill was a black metal box filled with charcoal with a well-worn rack placed on top, and on it were two whole fish. I was suddenly ravenous.

"What is that?" I said, leaning over the grill.

"They're called fish in these parts."

"Very funny." I shoved Ben with my hip and Fernando barked with excitement.

"Cooking is my hobby, even though I don't have a kitchen to speak of," Ben said. "You hungry?"

"Starving."

"Good. The fish is about done, and I made some pico de gallo and a little salad. I thought we'd take our plates up there and eat." He pointed up to a grassy spot, just above the house, that overlooked the water.

Ben set up a blanket and a couple of pillows for us, and I poured us both glasses of wine. He'd stuffed the fish with sliced lime, onions, and cilantro, and we ate greedily, licking our fingers. The sun was warm, and after a couple of glasses of wine I was feeling pleasantly fuzzy and about one step past inhibited.

"I feel like I know you so well even though we just met," I said. "But really, I don't know you at all. I know you're from L.A., you like to surf, and now I know you like to fish and cook, but I still don't know how you ended up here."

"I just like it here. I've been around the globe and this felt like a good place to stay awhile."

"I don't mean how you got here geographically. That I can understand. Believe me." I looked at him, wondering how much more I should say. "But what I mean is, why did you give it all up?"

"Give what up?" he said.

"Now you're just being coy." I waved my arms around us. "You know this isn't the typical way to live."

"Oh." He smiled. "You want to know why I don't work in an office somewhere. Why I don't wear real clothes and hold down a real job."

I worried that I'd insulted him. "Ben, there's nothing unreal about you, or your job. That's not what I meant. You made a huge decision to walk away from the world that most of us live in, and I just want to know how you knew it was the right thing to do."

Ben looked at me thoughtfully. "I caught my first wave when I was thirteen, and that was it for me. I felt like the water was where I was meant to be, and everything in between was just waiting."

"So did you go to high school?" I asked.

"Yes, I went to high school," he said teasing me again. "I've even read those things, what are they called? You know, they're made of paper, and sometimes there's a picture on the front?" He stretched out on his side and smiled up at me.

"You are infuriating, you know that? I think I like it better when you don't talk." I lay down on my side and faced him. "And I've seen your book collection, by the way. Eclectic."

"Snoop. Well, don't bother looking for my college diploma. I took off after my sophomore year and never went back. My dad didn't take the news so well. I haven't seen him in years." He paused for a second and ran one hand back through his hair. It was the first time I'd ever seen him look anything close to stressed.

"What about your mom?"

"Mom's different. She's a teacher and she respects that I'm a teacher, too. And she likes to travel, unlike Dad, so she's come to visit me. I've got a picture of her in the house. I'll show you."

I smiled. "I'd like that."

"Enough about me. You're always interrogating. Now it's my turn. Why are you here in Mexico all by yourself? You're a young, pretty girl. Shouldn't you be here with a boyfriend?"

This was the question I'd been waiting for. Why didn't I have an answer prepared? "Well, it's complicated," I said.

Ben made a buzzer sound. "Not good enough."

I sat up and poured us both another glass of wine.

"That bad?" He laughed.

I had so loved that Ben knew nothing about my old life, but it was time to stop hiding who I was from him. "I'm getting divorced." It was the first time I'd said it. In fact, it was the first time I knew it was certain. There was no going back.

Ben was silent, waiting for me to say more.

"It's all right," I said. "It's for the best. And this trip helped me realize it. So thank you for that."

"Mind if I ask what happened?"

"He cheated on me," I said flatly. "More than once. Most recently with one of my oldest friends."

"Ouch."

"And he's a really famous guy, so it was all over the press back home," I said. "That's why I left and came here."

Ben looked completely unfazed. "Do you still love him?"

"Yes. And there's a part of me that will always love him, even after what he did to me," I said. "But I'm not *in* love with him."

"Good. Want to go for a swim?"

We cleared the plates and blanket and dumped everything back in his house. Ben put a surfboard under one arm and took me by the hand with the other, and we walked down the hill to the water together. My cheeks were flushed, and I felt buzzed, but more from his touch than the alcohol. At the beach I took off my tunic and cutoffs and waded into the ocean. The sun beat down on the water, and the air was hot. I dunked my head under and when I came up I saw Ben putting the board in the water.

"You really want to surf right now?" I asked.

"Nah, just thought we'd sit on here and hang out. Come on up," he said.

We sat facing each other, each on opposite ends, straddling the board with our feet dangling in the water. We caught eyes and I felt like I was in high school, wanting the cute boy I was dancing with at the prom to kiss me.

"What is it, Gidget?" Ben said with a sly smile spreading across his face.

I pushed my body a couple of inches closer to his on the board and then he did the same.

"Why haven't you tried to kiss me yet?" I asked.

"Because I'm shy," he said.

"So am I."

We inched closer together again, this time our noses nearly touching.

"Well, I guess I'm not that shy," he said, and wrapped his arms around my waist, pulling me all the way to him, guiding my legs around him and gently kissing my lips. He pulled back and looked in my eyes, studying my face, and put his hand in my wet hair.

"That okay?" he said.

I nodded, unable to speak. He kissed me again, slowly, passionately. With his hand behind my head, he laid my body back onto the surfboard. He ran his fingers up and down my torso, tracing the curves of my body. My skin was suddenly covered in goose bumps, even in the heat. He arched his back and kissed my neck and my chest, and slid his hand behind my back, untying my bikini top. He moved it to the side and softly touched my nipples, then let his fingers trail down my stomach and gently touched me through the fabric of my bikini bottom. He lifted me back up and pressed my bare breasts against his chest, then whispered in my ear, "Let's go back to the house."

I followed him, my ability to speak completely paralyzed. In his little shack I stood at the edge of his bed, and the air was thick with humidity, like the tension between us. Without speaking, Ben pulled the string of my bikini bottom, letting it fall to the floor. Strangely, I felt at ease, not the least bit self-conscious as I stood there naked. Then he pulled off his shorts, and my eyes followed the blond arrow of hair that traveled from his navel down. Everything about him was perfect. *Everything.* We were nose to nose for a few moments, our bodies close but not touching, breathing in sync, as he played his fingers back and forth along my collarbone, then down my shoulders, and skimming over my breasts, and I felt him growing against me. I ran my hands over his biceps and down the funnel of his spine to the muscles at its base. He pulled the blanket back, and we lay down on the soft sheets, facing each other. He took my face in his hands, studying me the way he always did, and kissed me. He rolled on top of me, taking his time to kiss the nape of my neck, and nibble on my earlobes, then he made his way all the way down my body.

I felt totally uninhibited with Ben. He had a raw sexuality, and it was like we were two animals doing the most natural thing in the world. There was no choreography, no awkwardness. He tossed me around, flipped me over, sat me up, all with ease. He was giving, while also passionate and hungry, and my skin tingled as if we were making our own electricity.

We had sex for hours, only taking breaks to splash ourselves with cold bottled water. Ben surpassed any fantasy I'd had of him—this was nothing that I could have imagined. When we'd finally exhausted ourselves, the sun had set long ago, and we lay there staring at each other, by the light of one candle. The sound of waves crashed in the background, and a breeze picked up and whispered through the room. Ben was on his back with his arm stretched out, and I snuggled next to him, resting my head on his shoulder. Like so much of the time we'd spent together, there was no need for words, no need to make commentary or say anything at all, just sweet silence. We fell into a gentle sleep in each other's arms.

Just before dawn, Ben's alarm sounded. He reached over, pushed the button down, and propped himself up. "Good morning," he said softly, stroking the side of my face. "You look like an angel when you sleep."

"I can't believe you have an alarm clock." I buried my head in his shoulder. "That's a betrayal of everything you believe in."

"Not if it helps me catch a wave. You go back to sleep. I'm going to make some coffee." He lifted my head onto the pillow and slid out of bed.

I could see his silhouette through the sheer fabric of the curtain that divided his bedroom from the rest of the hut. I felt the giddiness of a schoolgirl as I watched him perform such a simple task as boiling water, measuring coffee, and filling his French press. I pretended this was my life, our life, waking up together and sharing a morning ritual. What if we lived in that house on the cliff and did this every day? Would I miss everything that I'd left behind—the glamorous surroundings, the staff, the endless bank account? Not only wouldn't I miss it, I realized, it didn't even feel real to me anymore.

Ben came back into the room, carrying a small tray with

the coffee and two cups. "You'll like this," he said as he poured me a cup. "I put a little cinnamon in with the beans."

"When do you have to leave?" I asked.

"Soon," he said. "I wish I could just stay here in bed with you, but I'll be back in a couple of days."

"That's okay," I said with a smile. "I can use the time to write. I think I finally have all the inspiration I need. What do you think of a story about a woman escaping from her past life to Mexico and falling in love with her hot surfing instructor?"

He leaned down and kissed me on the forehead. "Well, then come on, Danielle Steele, let's get you back to your computer. I'll drop you off on my way out of town."

~~~~~~

Ben and I kissed as he idled in front of the hotel. I reached back to pet Fernando. "Take care of Ben, you hear, Fernando? Don't let him flirt with any surfer girls. They won't scratch your ears as well as I do."

I walked into the hotel lobby with a lift in my step, and immediately I felt the eyes of the staff watching me. Did they see Ben drop me off, or could they just tell that something was different about me? I must have radiated happiness.

I hummed all the way back to my casita, and clicked my key card into the slot.

"Emma," said an all-too-familiar voice as I opened the door.

There, on the sofa in my casita, feet resting on the coffee table, was the last person on earth that I wanted to see. "Garrett, what the hell are you doing here?"

## 15

"Emma, where have you been all night? I've been worried about you. I was this close to calling the police." Garrett held up his thumb and index finger to show me a mere inch between.

I leaned my back against the door. This couldn't be happening. After the most perfect night of my life—the most meaningful night of my life—I wanted nothing more than peace and quiet to think about the last incredible twenty-four hours. Instead my heart was about to beat out of my chest. I sank to the floor and put my head on my knees. If I opened my eyes again, Garrett would be gone, I told myself, and I'd wake up and discover this was just an anxiety dream.

"Emma, talk to me. Come on, it's me over here. Did you think you could just run away and that would be it? I came all this way to see you, and I thought you'd be happy to see me. That maybe you'd miss me by now—the way I miss you."

I heard Garrett stand up and I raised my head from my knees and held one hand in front of me. "Don't, Garrett. Don't come over here."

"Emma, what the hell? Look at me. I've been sitting here all night just waiting for you, just to tell you how much I love you. And that's all you can say to me?"

I took a long look at him. He was unshaven, and not in his usual manicured way. His clothes didn't look all that fresh, either. He really had slept there on that sofa all night, I didn't doubt that. And then I looked in his big brown eyes, his brows raised in the center and knit together in a studied look of regret and sincerity. And then I thought, My God, he's acting. And he's not even very good at it. Gradually, my heartbeat began to slow. *Breathe, Emma.*

I stood up. "Garrett, I'll be back in a few minutes. Please don't follow me."

I went to the bathroom, slowly peeled off my clothes, and got in the shower. I turned on the water full blast and sank to the floor. I kept breathing, slowly, in and out. My panic was dissipating, but in its place there wasn't peace, only anger. That bastard. I'd gone from the most blissful night of my life to this. He missed me now? He had to see me now? How about calling first? How about asking permission?

But that was Garrett. It would never even occur to him to call. And it would never occur to him that I wouldn't melt into his arms when he showed up unannounced. Maybe that's why he looked so ragged right now. Nothing was going the way it was supposed to, and Garrett wasn't used to that. There was a whole staff of people whose job it was to make sure that everything went smoothly for him. I'd had my own people doing the same thing for me for the last seven years, and I'd gotten very used to it myself. Garrett hadn't known any other way of life for a lot longer than that, and I don't think he could even remember what it was like before the oceans of the world automatically parted for him.

I suppose that thought should have made me even angrier at him—I mean, the arrogance of showing up unannounced and expecting a warm welcome, after the way he had betrayed me? But instead I came to an important realization: This was the man I had married. He hadn't changed—I had. The girl he married followed him everywhere and was happy to hide safely in his shadow. I wasn't that girl anymore.

I let the water pour over me and then I stood and lathered myself with soap. I thought about Ben, and about the way he looked at me when I caught my first wave, throwing his arms up in the air and cheering me on. I thought about the way I felt up on the surfboard, that sense that I was floating on air, like I could conquer anything. That's the girl I was now, and I liked her. She still had a lot to learn, but she was headed in the right direction.

I turned off the shower, dried off, and put on cutoff jeans and a T-shirt. I walked out to the living room feeling bizarrely calm. It reminded me of that first day of surfing when I got hammered by wave after wave. Even while I was tumbling head over heels, my body knew what to do, and where to find the surface.

Garrett had his eyes closed when I walked in the room. "Hey," I said softly, wondering if he'd fallen asleep. I sat down on the other end of the sofa.

"I'm awake. Just resting my eyes. I didn't sleep so well last night."

I looked at him carefully. The sun was pouring into the room now and he looked tired. He also looked his age. The lines on his face that I'd always loved were set deeper, and I realized there was more salt in his thick peppery hair than I'd noticed before. None of it made him less attractive—I'd always thought he grew more handsome with age—but I remembered what he said the night of the Met Gala, about losing that part to a younger actor. Then I thought about Lily, and it struck me that Lily and he probably had a lot in common—more than Garrett and I did anymore. Not that I forgave her—but the notion gave me a little clarity.

"Why didn't you sleep in my bed last night?" I asked.

"I wanted to wait up for you. You're my wife, Emma. I worried about you out late, God knows where. What were you thinking? This is Mexico—you could have been kidnapped, anything could have happened to you."

I smiled. Yes, a lot can happen to you in Mexico. "Garrett, the last I heard from you, we were 'in different camps,' remember? And you told me I should get myself a lawyer."

"That's because you gave up on us, Emma. You broke my heart."

All right, that was it. I could be Zen for only so long. "Give me a break, Garrett. I broke your heart? You slept with my *friend.* And then when I confronted you, first you lied to me, and then you told me she wasn't the only one." My voice was starting to lift and crack. *Don't cry, Emma.* "And you have the nerve to say that I broke *your* heart?"

Dammit. Every bit of calm I'd found here was now gone. I'd thought I could hold it together and send him packing on the strength of all my newfound self-awareness. But seeing him here—the man I'd loved, my husband of seven years—

it killed me. I'd given myself to him completely. Had I been wrong? Or was I wrong now?

"I know. I know, Emma. I was wrong. And I'm ashamed of myself. It will never, ever happen again. I want to prove myself to you all over again. Let me win your heart back, Emma. You're the love of my life. You know that." He reached his fingers toward my hand and gently grazed my wrist. "You're still my wife," Garrett said. "And I'm still your husband."

It was like an out-of-body experience, listening to him talk and watching his facial expressions and gestures. It was all so familiar, like I'd seen it in a movie before (and I probably had).

I sighed. "I don't want to fight with you, Garrett."

He looked suddenly relieved, and I realized he'd completely misunderstood me. He thought I was coming around. But really I'd shut the door forever. He just couldn't see it, he couldn't fathom not getting his way.

My head was spinning and I felt a little sick. "Garrett, let's get some breakfast, okay? I need some air. And you could probably use some coffee."

"Do they eat eggs in Mexico?"

"They're called huevos," I said.

"Sounds good," he said, trying to sound lighthearted. "Maybe I'll even eat some refried beans."

I reached for my big sunglasses to hide my red-rimmed eyes, and we walked down the path to the resort's beachfront restaurant for breakfast. Garrett was trying to make small talk, commenting on the sounds of an exotic bird that was chirping above us, then pointing out an iguana sitting on a tree branch. I was silent. The restaurant was mostly empty and the staff buzzed about trying to look busy, but the few guests who were there all turned and looked as we walked to a table in the far corner. I'd been so invisible ever since I came here that I'd forgotten what it felt like to have your every move watched. For the first year that Garrett and I were together, I was always painfully aware of the way people looked at us when we were in public, trying to get a glimpse of the famous Garrett Walker or to snap a cell phone picture or eavesdrop on our conversation, so they could go home with a story to tell their friends about their brush with celebrity. It had made me deeply uncomfortable. But after a while I got used to it, and at a certain point I stopped noticing. That feeling of exposure just became a way of life. Right here, right now, it felt foreign to me again. I had relished my anonymity here. This was supposed to be my place of solace.

"Señora?"

"Oh, excuse me." I wondered how long the waiter had been standing there holding the pitcher of orange juice. "Yes, orange juice. Gracias."

We ordered breakfast. Garrett got bacon, eggs, and toast, I got my usual—a chorizo scramble and corn tortillas. While I ate, trying to savor each bite, Garrett was talking about a script he'd read on the plane ride. It was Bruckheimer's next movie, and it was looking good that he'd get the part. I watched Garrett as he spoke, and I found myself paying more attention to the way his mouth moved than to the words that were coming out of it. There was a desperate quality to the way he talked about the movie and I remembered again what he'd said the night of the Met Gala. *If I'm not an action hero, then what am I?* If he got this new film, he could put off answering that question a little longer, but sooner or later it was going to catch up with him. And it had nothing to do with age. On a basic level,

Garrett didn't have a clue as to who he was as a person. He'd never figured it out as a young man, and when he became a star, he never had to. Women wanted him, and men wanted to be him—and everyone wanted a *piece* of him. And that's how he derived his value. From being an object of desire. For the first time ever, I felt sorry for him.

He must have realized I wasn't listening. "You're somewhere else," he said to me.

I shook my head. "Sorry. I'm happy for you." He looked at me questioningly and I finished my thought. "About the Bruckheimer movie. I know you've been looking for something that could turn into a franchise. I hope you get it."

Garrett looked confused. He couldn't read my signals, so he wasn't sure what part he was supposed to be playing. "Emms, this isn't just good for me—this is good for us."

"Oh? How so?"

"My God, Emma." His face tightened in anger, as it had when I'd confronted him about Lily. I learned then that when you scratched Garrett's surface too deeply, he fought back. But not for the first time, Garrett surprised me. Instead of lashing out, he reached across the table and grabbed both of my hands, holding them together in his. He looked in my eyes just the way he had when he proposed all those years ago, and said, "Emma, I love you. Come home."

I felt so deeply sad in that moment, because I felt so cold. There wasn't a cell in my body that warmed to Garrett, and it was such a terrible shame. And such a waste. "Home?" I said. "Our *home* is no longer *home*. Garrett, you betrayed me. How would I ever trust you again? *Why* would I ever trust you again?" I pulled my hands out of his grip.

"Emma, I have . . ." He stopped, and I saw that his brown

eyes were swimming with tears. He swallowed. "I have loved you more than anyone. I've loved you the best, and the most, that I know how." He shook his head. "What can I do? Just tell me what to do, and I'll do it."

I guess I wasn't as coldhearted as I thought, because I felt tears welling in my own eyes. God, it killed me to see him sad. But I couldn't make him happy. I reminded myself: *I wasn't that girl anymore.* I believed him—he had loved me the best he could. But Garrett's best wasn't good enough. Maybe he wouldn't cheat on me with a friend again—he'd poisoned that well for good. But there would always be others, waiting in the wings, ready to give him the admiration he craved. And he'd probably think that if he kept it secret, and came home to me, and provided for me, that he was being a good husband. And by Hollywood standards, that might even be true. But those weren't my standards. And it wasn't even about the cheating. Not really. It was about being with someone who made you a better person, and for whom you *wanted* to be a better person. That wasn't Garrett for me. I was grateful to him, yes. He wasn't a villain, and I wasn't a victim. He'd never *tried* to hurt me, I knew that. And he really believed he'd done his best. But it was over.

"Garrett, I love you, and I always will. And I believe you when you say you love me, but I can't be married to you anymore." Tears were rolling down my face, and I pulled down my sunglasses to cover my eyes. Garrett's face registered grim understanding. Even his best wasn't good enough.

And just then, I saw him. Down the beach from the hotel was a man clad in black pants and a black T-shirt, with a long gray lens peering toward us.

"Jesus Christ, Garrett. You were followed." I got up and weaved through the tables of the restaurant.

Garrett caught up to me and put his arm around my shoulders. I wanted to bolt and run ahead of him, but I knew that would just cause more of a spectacle for the photographer. So I lowered my head and put one foot in front of the other. The walk back to my casita felt like I was crossing the Sahara in bare feet.

"Can I come in and get my bag?" Garrett asked when we reached my doorstep. "I need to call the pilot, too."

I didn't speak, but I held the door open behind me after I'd passed through. It was hard to believe that just a few hours ago I was practically floating through this door, and now I felt as if my feet were made of cinder blocks.

I sat on the bed and listened to Garrett make calls, first to the pilot to get his plane ready, then to the driver, and finally to the bellman. I heard the knock at the door and knew this was it. This was the final goodbye. My marriage was officially over.

"Goodbye, Garrett," I said, and gave him a tight hug. I surprised myself in that moment, because I discovered that I didn't want to let go. I knew it would be the last time he'd hold me. The last time I'd feel these familiar arms around me. This chapter of my life was closed.

"Goodbye," he whispered. I felt him shudder against me, and I knew he was crying, too. He took a deep breath, smelling my hair, and turned and walked out the door. The moment I heard the lock click, I fell in a heap to the floor, pressing my forehead to the rough fibers of the sisal rug, and let out a bellowing wail. I'm not sure how long I lay there crying, but I let it all out, and by the end I was spent.

Eventually I picked myself up and went to the bathroom to wash my face. There wasn't time to wallow. The photographer on the beach would probably stay on Garrett's trail, but where there was one photographer, more were sure to follow. There would be no more privacy or anonymity for me here. They'd be on me like flies, waiting for my tearful exit or another dramatic reunion—or to catch me with another man. I thought about Ben, and about photographers camping outside his home. I realized this place was sacred to me now, and I couldn't bear the thought of it—or Ben—being sullied by all that sniping and gossip that I'd left behind.

Ben was a dream. A wonderful, beautiful dream. And I couldn't let that dream turn into a nightmare. I needed to leave.

I called Grace. Typical of her, she asked me no questions and just went into crisp, calm problem-solving mode. She chartered a plane and said she'd meet me at Teterboro when I landed. She found out from Garrett's assistant that he was headed to L.A., so it was fine for me to go to the apartment. It was time to return to New York. It wasn't home anymore, but I had a job to do—a screenplay to write—and my mother hadn't raised me to be a quitter. And anyway, I was going to need the paycheck.

While packing my clothes, I found the T-shirt of Ben's I'd worn surfing that first lesson. Housekeeping had washed and folded it and stored it in a drawer. I picked it up and smelled it, and imagined that there was still a whiff of his particular scent—a mixture of sunblock, salt water, and sweat.

I held the T-shirt to me and sat down at the desk. I knew that leaving meant I'd never see him again. He'd said himself that this was the longest he had stayed anywhere since he dropped out of college, and his wanderlust was sure to engage again. Even if I thought that he and I had a future, by the time I came back he'd probably be gone, following the waves. I could follow him, I supposed, but how was that any different from following Garrett from location to location? It was just another crutch, and I needed to walk on my own. At least for a while. I could have stayed here with him forever, made a home up on that hill overlooking our beach. I could have written while he surfed, and every night we'd have each other. That was a lovely dream. But I was awake now.

I found some stationery in the drawer of the desk and started writing:

Dear Ben,

What can I say? That I completely fell for you, that by teaching me how to surf, you opened up a side of me that I never knew existed, that I learned more about myself in the short time I spent with you than I have in my entire adulthood?

Guess that's a start.

These days with you have been a dream, and I will forever miss you and hold you in my heart. Please know that I didn't want to leave like this, but real life intervened. I wish I could have told you goodbye. No, that's not true. I wish I never had to say goodbye.

Love,
Emma

I knew Ben wouldn't try to contact me. Even if he could track me down, it wouldn't be his style. I took one last look out at the water and imagined the sensation of riding a wave. That powerful ocean had healed me. My mom always told me, the Lord works in mysterious ways. If there's a God, I thought, she's big and blue, and I was lucky enough to have been held in her embrace. I kneeled in gratitude. "Thank you," I whispered.

The bellman's knock sounded at the door and that was it.

I left Ben's letter with the concierge and asked him to please give it to him personally. I didn't even try to hide the emotion on my face. I got into the waiting car.

We drove through modest little Sayulita. I saw a scruffy dog who reminded me of Fernando, and for a moment my heart did a flutter dance and my eyes combed the street for Ben. But no, it wasn't Fernando, and I knew that Ben was off surfing the groundswell. I hoped he was full of happiness. No one deserved it more.

Sayulita was behind us now, and we passed the road that led off to the little abandoned house on the cliff. I looked longingly down that curving road, to where my dreams resided.

# EPILOGUE

Fifty-fourth Street was a gridlock of black SUVs and limousines—I could just barely see the Ziegfeld theater in the distance. So close, and yet so far.

"Do you think anyone will mind if we're late?" My joke was all for show, and everyone knew it. This was not a night that I could be late. I surreptitiously (I thought) wiped my sweaty palms on the hem of my dress.

"Well, honey, they can't start your movie without you," Michael said. "And I know I didn't just see you using that Stella McCartney as a blotter."

I could never slip a thing past him. "I don't think they delay movie premieres for screenwriters, Mikey."

"That movie wouldn't exist if it weren't for your screenplay. And I don't know why we haven't drunk this yet." He gracefully uncorked a bottle of Dom Perignon and filled four glasses, one for each of us—Riley, Grace, Mikey, and me. "Emma, we are so proud of you. Here's to *Groundswell!*"

We clinked our glasses and sipped the champagne, and I hoped every single one of those bubbles would loosen the knot that I'd felt in my heart all day. This should be one of the most exciting, purely happy nights of my life—the premiere of my film that I'd poured my soul into writing—but instead I felt as if I'd lost something precious and irreplaceable.

That morning, I'd been walking through Soho on my way to a yoga class when I passed a building that reminded me so much of my old apartment with Garrett. I had a strange feeling of unreality, as if I'd been reminded of something that happened in a dream. Had it really been only a year since I said goodbye to that world? It felt like a lifetime ago. No, not just that. It felt like someone *else's* lifetime ago.

When I came back from Mexico, I should have been depressed and lost. But instead I flew into a creative whirlwind. I couldn't sleep, days blended into nights, and in three weeks the screenplay for *Groundswell* was done. The movie was my love letter to Ben, and I gave my characters the happy ending that Ben and I couldn't have in real life. My heroine stayed with her surfer, and she built her house on the cliff. It may not have been realistic, but I couldn't bear to write the scene where she walked away from him forever. And the movie was fiction, after all. I even set it in Costa Rica instead of Mexico because I wanted to keep Sayulita to myself—my sacred place.

I still longed for Ben every day, but I knew that I was right to leave Mexico when I did. If I'd learned anything from surfing, it was that there's no thrill like standing up on your own. If I'd stayed in Mexico it would have been too easy to lose myself in Ben's world the same way I'd lost myself in Garrett's. I needed to make a life for myself on my own terms. And that meant living alone, and writing my story.

It also meant firing my assistant. Grace had no trouble finding another job—on the strength of her talents and an enthusiastic recommendation from Michael, she was now working in PR for Carolina Herrera. And I found my dream apartment in Tribeca, in a modern building with great views, and a big kitchen where I was learning to cook more than just Grandma's country-fried steak. And yes, I'd gone on a few dates here and there, but nobody special. I'd sworn off actors or anyone in the entertainment business, and after a few bad experiences, I also swore off finance guys and lawyers. Grace said I was being too particular, and Riley said that if I crossed any more professions off my list, there wouldn't be any heterosexual men left in Manhattan.

Thanks to our prenup, my divorce from Garrett was quick and uncomplicated. Neither of us fed the rumor mill, but it was impossible to completely escape conjecture as to the cause for our separation, and Lily's name bubbled to the surface of a few gossip columns. I have it on good authority that Lily herself was most likely the source for the stories. It didn't get her anywhere, though. Last I heard, Garrett was dating a Brazilian model.

I saw Lily once. She started emailing me not long after I got back from Mexico, right about the time it became clear to her that Garrett wasn't looking for a long-term commitment—at least not with her. Finally I agreed to meet her for coffee. I let her apologize, and I forgave her. But I couldn't be friends with her anymore.

Once production on *Groundswell* started, I visited the set in

Costa Rica a few times. I loved watching the characters come to
life—even the surfer's little dog, Carlos (I changed all names
to protect the innocent). I had thrown all my creative energy
and focus into the script, and once I'd finished it, hanging
out on the set allowed me to hold on to the dream a little longer. Part of me still felt connected to its inspiration—as if that
door to my life weren't entirely closed yet.

I never talked about Ben, not even to Grace. But she wasn't
wrong when she said that I was too particular about the men
I dated. No matter whom I went out with, he suffered by com-
parison with Ben. The heartbreak for me—and the fact that
I would have to learn to accept somehow—was that I would
never meet anyone like him again. He came into my life for a
reason, and I was a better person for the experience. And now
I would have to find some way to put him behind me.

That morning a yoga class wasn't enough to distract me from
the knot of loss in my chest. But I had learned a lot about keeping my chin up in the last year, and going to the premiere was
important for my career. And I had my three best friends to give
me a kick in the seat of the pants if I needed it. Michael insisted
on coming over beforehand, just like the old days, to supervise
my preparation (I hadn't picked out my dress yet, and after all
these years, he still didn't trust me). As a surprise he arrived at
my apartment with Grace and Riley, plus three women dressed
in white uniforms—one with a massage table and two with suitcases of supplies—a chef with bags of groceries, and two stylish
(and fearful) young women with rolling racks of garment bags.

"You think we'd let you get ready for tonight *alone*?" Grace
asked. "Honey, we're just as excited about this movie as you
are."

"But it's only eleven a.m.," I laughed.

"Hi, I'm Michael, have we met?" Michael said, rolling his eyes. "Glamour takes time, doll face. Please tell me that I have taught you this much by now."

"We have massages, mani-pedis, and I brought my chef to cook us a healthy lunch," Riley said. "We need mimosas first, though. François?" Riley followed her chef into the kitchen in hot pursuit of her morning cocktail.

"Hair and makeup will be here later this afternoon," Michael said. "Now let's get working on everyone's looks for tonight."

Michael had the two assistants set up a makeshift showroom in my home office, displaying all the dresses, shoes, bags, and jewels as if we were in a boutique. In typical Michael fashion, one by one he styled each of us to his liking, obsessing over every detail. I must have tried on a dozen dresses before I saw that "a-ha" look come over his face, the same expression I'd seen him make since he was dressing me in college.

"That's it, Emma," he said. "That's the one."

It was a long, gold-sequined haltered Stella McCartney. It reminded me of the color of the beach as the sun first rose in the morning. It was perfect.

"I don't want to hear any whining that these Brian Atwoods are too high, Emms. Beauty is pain." Michael handed me a pair of strappy gold stilettos that must have had at least a five-inch heel. "And here's the correct clutch."

"I'll let you win on the shoes, but I need a bigger bag," I said.

"You only need lipstick, a credit card, and your phone, Emma. That bag's plenty big enough," he replied.

"Nope. Sorry, Michael," I said. "Gotta do bigger. Don't ask why."

Michael did his job well, and after the tornado of makeup

brushes, curling irons, and extensions subsided we were all spiffier versions of ourselves. I was glad to have my friends around me as we piled into the limo to head to the premiere of *Groundswell*. Drinking champagne with them didn't loosen the knot in my chest, but it did make me tremendously grateful for my blessings. I looked around at Michael, Grace, and Riley, and thought about how lucky I was to have them in my life. All smiling, laughing, and happy for me. It was good to know that I could stand on my own, but didn't have to be alone while I was doing it.

"You ready, Emma?" Grace said as we pulled up to the start of the red carpet, illuminated by a sea of flashbulbs. My pulse quickened and I closed my eyes and took a deep breath, letting it out slowly. Some things never changed.

"I guess so," I said. Then the car door opened and one of the publicists for the film, dressed in black and wearing a headset, was waiting to take me down the red carpet.

"Emma Guthrie has arrived," she said, pulling her microphone close to her mouth. "Good evening, Ms. Guthrie, right this way."

"Emma, Emma, Emma!" the photographers called out. "Right here! Look to your right! Over the shoulder Emma! Let us see the back of your dress!"

I walked past the interviewers without a sideways glance. Chances were, they would spend more time asking me about my divorce than about the film, and I wanted tonight to be about the movie, not me. I'd leave it to the actors to promote the film—they were way better at it. Once inside the theater, I breathed a sigh of relief, and we settled into our seats.

The lights dimmed and a hush fell over the crowd as the music began and sweeping views of the Costa Rican coastline lit up the screen. I felt a chill, and Grace gave my hand a squeeze. My stomach was flipping with nerves and excitement, and I think it was around a half hour into the film that I managed to take my first breath.

We'd found an unknown actor to play the Ben character, a young guy who'd grown up surfing. It helped that he was also ridiculously handsome. In his first scene, he emerged shirtless from the water, the sun just rising and glistening on his wet skin, and there was an audible gasp among the women in the audience, including me. But it wasn't the sight of the actor who played Ben that got to me the most. There could only be one Ben. No, what knocked me flat was the moment when the actress who played me got up on her surfboard the first time. My eyes filled, and I felt a few big teardrops roll down my cheeks.

The hair stood up on my arms, and I felt every bit of the joy of that scene—and more—because I remembered the moment it had happened for me. And the pure happiness I had felt washed over me so powerfully that the knot of loss in my chest finally loosened.

"Grace, I'm sorry, I have to go," I whispered in her ear.

"What? Are you okay?" Her brow wrinkled in concern.

"Yes, don't worry about me." I smiled. "I'm more okay than I've ever been."

I whispered goodbye to Riley and Michael and snuck out of the film. In my sky-high stilettos, I ran over to Fifth Avenue and hailed a cab.

"JFK, please," I said to the driver. "As fast as you can get me there." If the cabdriver thought there was anything strange about a woman with no luggage and a couture dress in a rush to get to the airport, he didn't show it.

I looked in my not-so-little clutch and smiled down at my passport. I knew I'd been carrying that thing around for a reason. For the last year, every time I left the house, I made sure I had it with me. I knew it was silly—it's not as if I really would drop everything and jet off to God knows where (would I?). But it reminded me of everything I'd learned from Ben, and it gave me a feeling of optimism and adventure whenever I caught sight of it in my bag. Even if I didn't drop everything—I knew that I could. The choice was mine, and so were the consequences.

"I need a ticket to Puerto Vallarta on your next flight," I said to the woman at the Mexicana airlines desk.

She looked me up and down, and raised a curious eyebrow. "No luggage?"

"It's a last-minute trip," I said. "When is the next flight?"

"There's a red-eye that leaves in an hour," she said. "If you go to the front of the security line, you can probably make it."

My five-inch-heeled torture chambers slowed me down, and it's a miracle I didn't break my neck racing to the gate. But I made it, and once on the flight I nestled into seat 37B and immediately kicked off my shoes. I was so happy that I didn't even care that I was in a middle seat in coach, sandwiched between a linebacker on one side and a Chatty Cathy on the other. I made up a story about lost luggage and a high school reunion, and then closed my eyes and feigned sleep.

<hr />

"Señora, we are here," the cabdriver said.

"Sí, gracias," I said, and handed him a wad of cash.

If you had asked me in that moment what I was there for, I'm not sure what I would have said. I'm not sure I knew. I'd had a long plane ride to ponder the question, and I still didn't really have an answer.

I got out of the cab and shook out my hair. The sun was on the verge of peeking over the horizon, and the water was barely visible, but I could smell it. I took off my shoes for the last time and set them at the edge of the sand. I pressed my grateful toes into the fine grains of the beach, and felt the wind whip my dress around my legs.

Then I heard two precious sounds. The strongest was the crashing of the waves. The second, less distinct, was a happy bark. As I walked, the bark grew louder and a familiar scruffy form raced toward me across the beach. At the edge of the water was a surfer, his back to me. He turned at the sound of his dog barking, and I saw a smile slowly creep across his face. I'm not sure how much time passed while Ben and I walked toward each other, but I know that neither of us rushed.

"Well, hello, Gidget," he said, once we were a hand span apart.

"Hi there, Surfer." I smiled.

Then he took me in his arms. His wet ocean hair touched my lips, and I tasted salt. The rising sun warmed my face, and the answer to my question came to me: I was there because there wasn't another place in the world that I'd rather be.

# ACKNOWLEDGMENTS

Writing this book has been the realization of a lifelong dream. I had always wanted to try my hand at fiction, but was never brave enough to take it any further than creative writing classes. Finally, (finally!), I did it, but not without the help and encouragement of a few key people.

Thank you so much to Jen Bergstrom, my amazing publisher, and Tricia Boczkowski, the greatest editor ever. The two of you have believed in me and supported me from day one. You took a leap of faith that a girl who specializes in cheeseburger recipes could write a novel, too.

My team at William Morris Endeavor, especially my literary agent, Andy McNicol, who helped me so much throughout this process, thank you! Also, a BIG thanks to my publicist, Keleigh Thomas.

Kate White, the wonder woman editor-in-chief of *Cosmopolitan* and bestselling novelist, encouraged me to write fiction, and shared her how-to tips and knowledge with me. I am so grateful to you for your support!

Much, much gratitude goes out to Peternelle Van Arsdale, who has probably read and re-read this book as many times as I have. Thank you so much for all of your critiques and guidance.

For early reads and your thoughts, thank you Kelli Morgan, Beth Stern, Chris Clarke (you get extra credit), and Ricky Paull Goldin. Also thanks to Mark Mullett and Keith Bloomfield.

Billy Joel, the best ex-husband a girl could ever ask for, thank you for always being there for me.

Special thanks to the Four Seasons Punta Mita and their staff for an incredible stay during the time I spent in Mexico researching this book. The margaritas and guacamole totally helped get the creative juices flowing. Seriously, the best working trip ever.

And last but certainly not least, thank you, Mom, for being the strong woman that you are and telling me when I was a kid that I could do anything I wanted. You gave me the confidence to do this!